Susan,

Thanks for
supporting my
writing!

Taylor L.

Old Money, Old Secrets

Kyle Cornelius

For information contact Triton Press/Nautilus Publishing, 426 South Lamar Blvd., Suite 16, Oxford, MS 38655.

ISBN: 978-1-936-946-31-0

Triton Press
A division of The Nautilus Publishing Company
426 South Lamar Blvd., Suite 16
Oxford, Mississippi 38655
Tel: 662-513-0159
www.nautiluspublishing.com

First Edition

Front cover by Vaughn Design

Library of Congress Cataloging-in-Publication Data has been applied for.

10   9   8   7   6   5   4   3   2   1

To Mom, who gave me a love for books

1

April 14, 1865.
Ford's Theater, Washington, D.C.

"This is it. Steady and true." The man could hardly keep his hands from shaking. His palms were sweaty. His heart raced. He was to meet his contacts in the basement bar of the building adjacent to the theater. He walked slowly and deliberately down the subterranean hallway, attempting with little success to calm his unsteady nerves. He licked the palm of his hand, tasting the salt of his own sweat, and ran it over his dark, curly hair. He had a stylish mustache that drooped slightly over the corners of his mouth and was dressed as if he was going out for a night on the town with a wide rippling tie tucked underneath his vest.

"Alright, you know what to do, you've been over it hundreds of times," he thought to himself as he pulled the cuffs of his shirt so they would project from under his jacket sleeve. He opened the jacket and felt for the Derringer. It was there, in place, loaded. As he neared the door to the Star Saloon he paused and looked at his pocket watch. It was a little early yet, but he could not bear a moment more of waiting. He tucked the tail of his shirt more tightly into his trousers, buttoned the top button of his jacket, changed his mind and unbuttoned it, and rolled his shoulders back for a moment before relaxing. He took a deep breath through his sharp nose and exhaled slowly through his mouth, looked at the floor, and then closed his eyes. When he looked back up he was still, he felt alert, and he appeared to be calm and collected. He was, after all, an actor.

He was about to walk through the open door when he heard something astounding from inside the room.

"Are you that dense, Corbett? It's too goddamn convenient. He won't last another week. It's not going to be much of a trial."

"Don't use the Lord's name in vain in my company if you want to keep it, especially on Good Friday. The recklessness of your speech is abhorrent to the ears of God. He doesn't know enough to compromise us, does he?"

"No, and spare me your preaching for once. Even if he did know something, who would believe him? Nobody is going to trust a word that sumbitch says anyway."

"You know how much of a braggart he is."

"Doesn't matter. After tonight he might as well be Judas Iscariot."

The man didn't know what to think. A Judas? Never. Not him. He would take his place in history as a liberator, not a murderer. What did these two really think about the president? John Wilkes Booth was so sure that this was the right thing to do, but was he being used as a knife in the hand of a larger Brutus? In his mind Lincoln and the radicalism that he fertilized and rode into power was responsible for the mindless ravaging of the South, murder on an unprecedented scale, and the desecration of the Constitution. He was a man who openly blasphemed against the natural order of God, vowing to make the races equal. Despot of despots, intent on crossing the Rubicon like Julius Caesar and overthrowing the grand Republic. It was not only politically advantageous, it was Booth's moral crusade to eliminate this man.

He must first get himself out of whatever maligned situation that he was in. A well of anger and conviction surged up inside of Booth that buttressed his confidence and he strode into the bar room. It was not very well lit, just a few lanterns burning on each end of the bar and hanging in the four corners. The brick walls offered no ventilation save two windows near the top of the right wall that were tilted open slightly. The air inside the room held a bit off a chill. Booth had been here many times, often after plays that he acted in at Ford's Theater. A short candle flickered in the center of the table against the far wall where two men sat. He walked up boldly and nodded. "Boston, Everton." He pulled out a chair and sat down.

The two men smiled back easily. One of them was Boston Corbett, a strange, fiery, and pious man of slight build. Born Thomas Corbett, he was a drifting alcoholic until an encounter with a Salvation Army street preacher in Boston led him to a born-again experience. He was so profoundly moved that he changed his name, following the example of Christ when He renamed Saul and at the same time paying tribute to the city where he had seen the light. Corbett then took it upon himself to spread the Gospel and energetically chastised his fellow man on street corners for their sins, warning of the inescapable hell fire that surely awaited the impenitent. He grew his hair long in impersonation of Jesus and wore it parted down the center. To resist the animalistic temptations that threatened his righteousness, one summer night before the war he carefully castrated himself with a pair of scissors, attended a prayer meeting, ate a meal, and only then did he allow himself to seek medical treatment. Despite the absence of his virility, Corbett was known for an unflinching sense of duty in his service to the US Army. He had a stark conception of morality that allowed for no gray area and believed that the Lord's hand guided his every action. He was a survivor of the Andersonville prison camp, where he had continued to preach to prisoners and captors alike in a holier-than-thou fashion. After a prisoner exchange he spent three weeks recovering and returned to the ranks of the Army, more convinced than ever that he held some sort of divine favor.

The other was Everton J. Conger, a former dentist from Ohio turned cavalry officer. After recovering from near-fatal battle wounds, he was reassigned to work directly for the federal government in Washington. He was meticulous, domineering, and often crass. After narrowly escaping death and witnessing so many others, he had come to accept the inevitability of dying and the cruelty of its timing. He was now cold to it, unfeeling and uncaring, and unlike Corbett, doubted that there was a heaven waiting on the other side. He remembered the smallest details—how a person's nose twitched to one side, the slant of the letters in someone's penmanship, a scratch on the back of their hand. Truthfully, he was saddened by the thought that the war was coming to a close and feared that the future would not be as gratifying for him. Thwarting the ever-looming presence of imminent danger was a feeling that he had grown fond of and briefly gave him the titillation of immortality. For the past year he had been a spy.

"Good evening, John," began Conger. "This is a night that will live forever."

"Undoubtedly. We shall be heroes of legend, the saviors of the empire. I say to you that we shall never allow the seeds of dictatorship be sown on our native soil," Booth replied.

Corbett nodded approvingly. "Absolute authority rests only on the throne of The Almighty."

"Should we go over it one last time?" asked Conger.

Booth shook his head. "I'm prepared… You?"

"Poised as a Spartan," Conger smiled back.

"Good. Where will you go? The radicals will want someone's head on a platter."

"Its best that I stay in Washington, we need to keep our ears open. Plain sight is often the most convenient and unassuming place to hide," said Conger.

Booth smirked and looked at his hands as he laid them on the tabletop, lacing his fingers together. "How many others do you think we can count on after tonight?"

Corbett shot Conger a glance, expecting him to have a quick answer. "We are mostly alone for now. According to the men at the top, this operation doesn't exist," Conger said.

"If discovered we are on our own, but if not, we will be witness to the greatest age of liberty that mankind has ever known. Others will recognize our heroism and be inspired to stand on the side of rectitude. The government must be returned to the people," added Corbett.

"As it shall be," replied Booth. "The original intent of our nation's founding will not be suffocated and divine providence will once again light our path."

Corbett looked at Booth like he was his disciple, but something about him wasn't entirely genuine. Something in Corbett's cheeks and the way his mouth turned up just so slightly seemed forced, unnatural. Conger radiated a haughty confidence with a well-practiced poker face. Booth smiled at them both for a few moments without speaking, feeling his chest tighten and his heart begin to race. A muffled eruption of laughter was heard through the walls from the audience next door. Booth took the watch out of his front jacket pocket and flipped it open. "Well… just a little while longer." He felt the nerves in his hand begin to tingle and shoved the watch back into his pocket before his hand started shaking. "Would you two like a drink?" he asked.

"I wouldn't mind one," replied Conger.

"I find my strength in the Lord," said Corbett, "but if you feel so inclined, go right ahead."

Booth stood up and walked behind the bar. He knew where the whiskey was. His legs felt heavy and he became self-conscious. Corbett and Conger were watching him, friendly faces that hid an advanced sensory perception and a knowledge that he could not know, something sinister he had yet to recognize for himself. They were like hounds, and he the prisoner that had made friends with them in a crowded, lonely place. He imagined a fugitive, tracked down by the same hounds that he had once loved. And as Booth looked at them, he could almost see their faces contort, wet black noses and long floppy ears.

He took a half empty bottle and two squat glasses and returned to the table. He poured twice and slid a glass toward Conger, who smiled without showing his teeth and looked into Booth's eyes in a knowing way, like his boarding school roommate after they had both gotten away with something. Conger raised his glass, "To freedom from tyranny." Booth touched his glass to the rim of Conger's and they drank. Booth swallowed with an unintended grimace and then coughed and laughed uneasily. He looked across the table; they looked back at him.

•••

Booth stood behind the door to the viewing box where the president sat. Corbett and Conger waited down the hall at the head of the stairs, watching him. He was beginning to perspire under his suit. "They aren't your friends," he kept telling himself. "They've played you. They will have no use for you after this." He couldn't walk out; they wouldn't let him. He was trapped when he walked into the bar room and now he realized it.

Booth looked at the brass doorknob. Behind it awaited the moment he had longed for, the moment he had fantasized over so many times. He was afraid, but how could he let this opportunity slip through his fingers? Was he willing to sacrifice himself for the greater good? He knew the answer, as reluctant as he might be. It was predetermined.

He slowly wrapped his fingers around the doorknob—it was warm and a little greasy. He stood there for a moment unwilling to turn it. Booth turned his head and glimpsed the hounds staring back at him like a piece of meat that they were ready to devour. There was no escape the way he had come. His eyes turned back towards the doorknob where his hand trembled. He knew what he must do. He had to live up to the moment, possess the heroism that he portrayed on stage. It was his time to place himself amongst the company of Macbeth and Henry V. This was his defining performance.

The door opened effortlessly and quietly and there he sat, right in front of him. Abraham Lincoln teetered on the edge of an upholstered rocking chair with his hands on the balcony railing, leaning forward to get a better view.

An actress bantered across the stage and Lincoln hooted and then glanced at his plump, smiling wife Mary Todd as if the situation acted out below was somehow parallel to their own personal life. His black beard was neatly trimmed and beginning to show a little gray, and his wrinkles were deepened from the burden of the past four years. In the early hours of the morning he had grieved until he felt hollow. The war was recently won, and the nation reunited, but he could never bring back all the lives of the men that had been lost. Fathers, sons, husbands, brothers—all had sacrificed and he had directed that sacrifice. Ahead lay the arduous task of rebuilding, but tonight was for entertainment and well deserved relaxation and the theatre was a temporary respite from carrying the weight of the world. How he had looked forward to this; *Our American Cousin* was touted as the funniest comedy running and he had yet to see it. Lincoln scooted back in his chair and craned his neck tentatively, his long narrow head rising above the others there. Besides Lincoln's wife, there was a youthful, handsome Union Army officer and a young lady that accompanied him.

The play was about to reach the line that always drew the most uproarious laughter from the audience. For Booth, it was the opportune moment. He raised the Derringer and put his other hand on the hilt of a knife that was sheathed in his belt. His finger was on the trigger, lightly applying pressure.

"Don't know the manners of good society, eh? Well, I guess I know enough to turn you inside out, old gal, you sockdologizing old man-trap."

The audience thundered and Booth fired. Through a cloud of blue smoke Booth could see the president collapsed forward onto the railing. His legs sprawled backwards on the floor of the box and his head was red with blood. Terrified screams filled the theater. Booth pulled out his knife and stabbed at the army officer as he lunged towards him, cutting down hard and opening a deep gash in the young man's forearm. The officer recoiled and Booth stabbed at him again, the blade glancing off his chest. Booth looked back, expecting to see Corbett rush into the box with his gun drawn, but the doorway was empty. He shoved the young officer and vaulted over the railing towards the stage. As he fell, his riding spur was caught on a decorative flag hanging from the president's box, altering his trajectory. He landed awkwardly and his left foot slipped out from under him. Booth fell to one knee but quickly stood back up, adrenaline coursing through his body.

He looked out at the screaming, confused crowd and knew just the line to use. He thrust his knife high, slicing through the air above him. "Sic Semper Tyrannis!" he shouted. *Thus always to tyrants.* He rushed offstage behind the set, crashed through a back door and sprinted out into the alley behind Ford's Theater. There was a stable across the alley and a boy was there holding Booth's horse for him as he had been instructed to do earlier.

"Didn't expect you coming from that way," said the boy. "Why you in such a hurry?"

Booth mounted the horse and kicked her forcefully twice, yelling "Hyah! Hyah!" The horse bolted and they careened down the alley, turned a corner, and took off into the night. The boy looked after them dumbfounded.

Conger and Corbett were ready to intercept Booth in the hallway outside of Lincoln's box. They had both smiled perversely when they heard the gunshot and reached for their pistols. Seconds passed and Booth did not come out. There was noise, calamity, hysteria; he had gone through with it alright. A full minute passed as they waited and still Booth didn't show. Conger looked at Corbett and raised his right eyebrow. He motioned with his pistol that he was going inside and Conger burst through the door of the box shouting "My President! My President!"

"Who did this!?" Conger asked the army officer.

"I'm not sure. He was gone so quickly I wasn't able to tell who he was. He is gone, sir." The young man sat on the floor cradling his beloved leader and began to sob.

Conger looked behind at Corbett and then glared down at the stage in disbelief. They had been foiled. Conger regained his composure. "We must find a doctor. Boston come with me! We have to find a doctor immediately!" The two men dashed out of the box, through the hallway, and stomped down the stairs hurriedly.

"Where'd he go?" Corbett asked

"He jumped, you idiot!" Conger barked as they ran down the stairs.

They burst out of the theatre into the back alley where an unorganized group of men were frantically trying to decide what to do. They came up behind them and there was a man in the center who had the stable boy by the collar of his shirt. "Which way did he go?!" screamed the man as he shook the terrified boy.

The boy pointed down the alley, "That way! He took off that way on his horse!"

The hot-headed man bashed the boy impulsively on the side of the head, threw him to the ground, and he and some other men ran off in the direction that the boy had pointed. Conger knelt down beside the boy as he lay there dizzy and bleeding from scrapes on his hands. "Are you alright? Can you stand?" he asked.

"Yes," muttered the boy. Conger took him by the shoulders and helped him to get to his feet.

"That fellow ought not have hit you like that. Are you hurt bad?"

Other men gathered around the boy who blinked a few times and shook his head. "Naw sir, I don't think so. Why'd he do that?"

"The president is inside the theatre and somebody shot him. Did you see a man run out this way?"

"Booth, you know, the actor. He come running through that door there and hopped on his horse that my boss told me to keep for him. 'You in a hurry,' I says and he didn't even look at me. He jumped on that horse and took off. He went down the alley and turned in the street... That's all I saw. I want to sit down."

Conger let go of the boy and he stumbled over and sat on the ground with his back resting on the brick wall of the theater.

"You will be fine son, the Lord has you in his care," said Corbett. The pair walked down the alley and into the nighttime streets of Washington. The moon was out and they could see the outline of the unfinished dome of the Capitol building in the sky to the southeast.

"We've got to find him. He can't talk," said Corbett.

"He doesn't know who to trust. He isn't going to admit to being the man who shot the president yet. We'll find him, we'll find him before anybody else does. I can promise you that."

•••

April 18, 1865
Charles County, Maryland

Booth sat under a thick oak tree in the swamp where he was hiding.

He'd been using a red appointment book as a diary and he propped it on his right knee as he wrote. He was careful to move as little as possible because he had broken his left leg during the jump and it would sear with white hot pain at the slightest movement after he had gotten settled. It was getting hotter and more humid as spring blossomed and mosquitos were his constant companion.

He wrote down his thoughts quickly and furiously. He knew now that he had been used, been the willing fool. The reasons why were so obvious after the fact. Now they would have their glorious coup d'état and everyone would assume that it was more or less a natural succession. Booth winced from the pain of his left leg and blotted a period on the end of the last sentence. Someone had to know about the real conspirators, the fight for southern independence must continue. He was unwilling, unable, to give up on that ideal.

He heard hooves on the road a hundred yards behind him through the woods. He tried the best he could to make himself small, and painfully turned his body to hide behind the trunk of the thick oak. The hoof beats stopped and Booth's heart began to pound as he fought back panic.

"What?" a voice asked.

"Nothing, thought I saw something."

"You want to get off and take a look?"

"Nah, it was nothing. Let's go."

The horses started up again and their sound grew faint within a few minutes. Booth let out a long breath and then began to suck air heavily. He reached for the diary on the ground under his legs and turned to the page where he had begun writing that day. It was imperative that he get this written truth as far away from him as he could. If they found him with it they would just destroy it. He carefully tore out each of the day's pages from the binding and laid them in a neat stack on a knotted root.

He would give the pages to Thomas Jones to mail. Thomas could get the package through for him. Jones had been helping Booth evade capture in the swamp and brought him provisions and newspapers so he could read of the manhunt for himself. His fame had grown monumentally overnight, but instead of being congratulated and revered, here he was—stinking, tired, injured, and on the run. Booth took the loose pages and tucked them back into the red book and put the book inside his jacket.

•••

April 22, 1865
New Orleans, Louisiana

Captain J.C. Mason was glad to be on land for a few days. His vessel, the S.S. *Sultana*, was one of the finest steamboats on the Mississippi River, but the trip had worn him down. They had just come downstream from Cairo, Illinois bearing bad news. On the upper reaches of the river the people took it with a feeling of absolute loss and exasperation, as if their own father had died, but down here fellas weren't so mournful. The president of the United States, Abraham Lincoln, had been assassinated only a week before. The *Sultana* was decorated all over with black crepe paper, signaling the great loss of a nation, or half of it anyway.

The assassination really didn't weigh too heavily on Captain Mason's mind. What did bother him though, was the fact that he knew the man they said had shot Lincoln, John Wilkes Booth. He had met Booth a few years earlier on a visit to the East Coast. They were introduced by a mutual friend and really hit it off and had kept fairly regular correspondence ever since. Booth had even bought into Mason's most recent endeavor, the purchase of the *Sultana*.

The *Sultana* was magnificent, a large sidewheeler with gorgeous woodwork. Tall smokestacks billowed black soot into the air from her mighty boilers and the large paddle wheels on each side of the ship pounded the water with steady, unrelenting rotations. There were two decks that circled the ship, one upper and one lower, with intricate lacy railing. The passenger cabins were luxurious, and a large hold below decks carried cargo of all sorts. At the top was the wheelhouse where the captain surveyed the mighty river and directed the imposing vessel with quiet, instinctual concentration.

The night before had been a wild one. Even though J.C. Mason did not partake as heavily as his crew, or in the same establishments, he did partake nonetheless. He had gone to a bar in the Quarter that catered to the professional set. It was frequented by the Union officers that occupied the city as well as boat captains, lawyers, and merchants that had cut lucrative contracts to supply the blockade ships anchored just a short way out into the Gulf of Mexico. Mason had walked back to the *Sultana* in high spirits at midnight after an imported cigar, Jamaican rum, and a winning poker game. New Orleans was probably the only place in the South where you could find such indulgent vices at this point. While the rest of the South was reeling from the damages of total war, New Orleans had already started the rebuilding process. Because it had come under Union control so early, many people in New Orleans enjoyed the wealth that came imported with the U.S. Army. The sanitation of the city had actually improved under the occupation, though most of the city's elite were less than pleased about having hoards of teenaged Yankee soldiers policing the streets. When Mason got to the *Sultana* he went to his cabin and lay down on his bed, thankful for the opportunity for a good, unimpeded rest.

When he awoke the next day he dressed in his uniform, blue coat and white hat, and walked up busy Canal Street to the partially completed United States Customs House. It was a grand building, several stories tall, and sort of Egyptian-looking thought Mason; when it was finished it would really be something. He strode through the door. There were several men in blue uniforms inside busily hustling about. Only the first floor was occupied due to the unfinished construction. He walked over to the front desk where a bespectacled clerk was sitting and said "J.C. Mason, captain of the SS *Sultana*. We arrived yesterday evening." The clerk directed him to an office where he did all the required paperwork for his vessel, then walked back into the main lobby.

As he headed towards the door to leave, the clerk called, "Captain Mason, before you go, there was a package delivered here with your name on it." He reached under the counter and produced a small package wrapped in brown paper and tied up with twine. "It must be yours." On the wrapping was written: *J.C. Mason, Captain of the SS Sultana, United States Customs House, New Orleans, Louisiana.*

"For me, huh?" the captain said as he took the package, a little surprised. It wasn't heavy. "Thank you." He turned and walked out onto Canal Street.

•••

April 26, 1865
Garret Farm, Rural Virginia

"Booth! Come out with your hands where we can see them! This is your last chance!" yelled Federal Detective Everton J. Conger from outside the door of the tobacco barn. Fire from the soldier's torches glowed orange against the darkness of the night.

"You won't take me!" shouted Booth from inside. The walls of the barn were beginning to be licked by the flames coming off of the straw that had been piled around its base. "I am an instrument in the hand of God himself!" He could see the soldiers gathered around the door through the spaces between the wooden slats of the barn wall.

"You won't make it out of this alive Booth! You can stay in there and burn to death like a dog or you can come out and face trial like a man. Drop all of your weapons and come out now!" shouted Conger.

Booth could feel the flames growing around him, the fire getting closer and hotter. *So this is how it ends*, he thought to himself and coughed from the smoke. He was proud past the point of vanity, and although he was in an extremely low condition, to Booth it seemed rather glorious. One thing was certain, he wouldn't go down without a fight. He would take as many as he could down with him.

He dropped his crutch and with all the strength in him, adrenaline flowing, Booth began to make his way towards the door unaided. His broken leg slowed him but he did not feel it, nor did he care. If this was to be his last stand it would be full of fury. With one arm he raised his carbine and with his other hand gripped a pistol that was shoved into his belt. Suddenly a shot cracked through the air and he fell to the ground, his body draping unnaturally onto the dirt floor. Booth tried to move, begging to find life in his limp limbs, but discovered that he could not.

Outside, the soldier who had fired gave a loud shout. "He's down! He's down! I got him! The Lord Almighty guides my hand!" It was Boston Corbett perched in a shooting position on one knee. He stood up and wielded the rifle over his head with both hands. "Like a stone in the sling of David!"

Booth wasn't coherent. He lay there on the porch of the farmhouse with his eyes closed, still as the grave, bleeding and struggling for breath. His arms and legs were completely paralyzed. When he finally did open his eyes Conger was crouched over him. "There he is. He's coming to," said Conger. "Search him! Take everything he has. It could all be evidence."

Two privates followed the orders with rough motions. They dug through Booth's pants pockets, tossing over his limp body like a rag doll. Booth's face was pressed against the dusty porch, dark red blood mixed with spinal fluid flowing faster onto the roughhewn boards as they searched.

"Nothing here sir," said one of the soldiers to Conger.

"Roll him back over and keep looking," he responded.

The soldiers rolled up his pants legs and found a knife strapped to his right calf, then they took his shoes off.

"Search the coat," Conger ordered.

One of the privates pulled the coat from Booth's body; his arms flopped out of the sleeves and landed on the porch with a dead thump. The soldier recovered a plain little red book from inside the jacket and handed it Conger. Conger stood up and flipped through it from cover to cover. He couldn't believe it. That little shit. He flipped all the way through again backwards.

"Leave us," he said. The privates saluted and turned on their heels and walked back towards the barn.

Once they were out of earshot, Conger crouched down again and jeered condescendingly, "So why'd you do it John?"

"You won't… get away… with this," Booth whispered with as much strength as he could muster.

"It looks like it's you who didn't get away with it. Where are the missing pages?" he demanded quietly.

"I don't…" Booth's throat gurgled, "know."

Conger shook the red book in Booth's face. "The diary! There are pages missing! Who has them?"

Booth coughed up blood. Conger reached back and smacked Booth hard across the face with the diary. "Where are they?"

Booth was silent, his head rolling to the side.

"Tell me or I will kill you right now."

"Tell my mother I died for my country," Booth whispered, looking away. "Raise my hands."

"What?"

"I want to see my hands."

Conger picked up Booth's forearms and dangled his limp hands in front of his face.

"Useless, useless," Booth murmured.

Conger dropped Booth's arms. "Where are the pages, damnit?"

Booth stared ahead lifeless, his eyelids beginning to slowly droop down. Conger grabbed Booth by the shoulders and shook him. "Answer me!" Booth's head rolled around unimpeded by muscle resistance. His breathing had stopped. Conger put his finger on Booth's neck and felt for a pulse. Nothing. He was dead.

"God damn it!" Conger ejected forcefully. He stood up, muscles tense, and breathed out heavily in frustration. He reached down and picked up the diary and opened it; maybe there would be some clues in the pages that were left. A loose piece of paper fell out and drifted onto Booth's corpse. Conger picked it off of the blood-soaked shirt and read silently to himself.

J.C. Mason, Captain of the S.S. *Sultana*,

       I assume you got the package. I could not think of an abler man to send it to. I trust you with it as I would trust you with my life. Guard it and I will meet up with you in St. Louis after this is all over. Do not speak of it to anyone yet, as the information contained within those pages is very dangerous and should be handled delicately and with the utmost care and precision.

                                        J.W. Booth

Conger smiled to himself. "Well John, it seems you didn't need to tell me after all. We appreciate your services." He folded the unsent letter and put it in his pocket.

The dawn was breaking. Conger mounted his horse and rode all day until he reached Washington, stopping only to cross the Potomac and to commandeer a fresh horse from a lonely traveler. He reached the offices of the United States Intelligence Service and found the telegraph operator slumped at his desk, half asleep. "This is urgent! Telegraph all of our agents along the Mississippi and tell them to find J.C. Mason and this boat the *Sultana*. They are to eliminate him and any belongings that he may have with him."

"Yes sir!" said the startled man. He turned and began to tap away on the telegraph.

•••

April 27, 1865
The Mississippi River near Memphis, Tennessee

Captain Mason looked out from the helm at the powerful river in front of him, its huge brown current working against him on their upstream journey. He had thought before that maybe he had bitten off more than he could chew, but now, alone, the uncertainty clouded his mind like a thick fog.

There wasn't a free nook or cranny on the entire river boat. Men were stacked on board like cord wood, their thin, sickly bodies pressed up against one another. There were soldiers crowded up and down the stairwells, underneath the deck, into every cabin, and anywhere and everywhere that there was any extra space to be had. They hung over the railing and it was all many of them could do to keep from being forced overboard.

The scene was an awful one and the smell so offensive that Mason wished he could just sew his nostrils shut. Many of the POWs were racked by dysentery, worms, and other forms of sickness and pestilence. The proud ship was now transformed into a floating, stinking mass of human decay and anguish. These were men that were thought of more as cattle than as men at all to many, especially to the officers of the prisons, and even to their superiors in the Union Army. It was hard for Mason not to feel sympathy for these disheveled men and their terrible plight, but in the back of his mind horror stories of the Northern prison camps kept arising. Seeing this sight first hand however, picking sides lost much of its meaning for him. Despite this, he still had a business to run.

The truth was, being the ever-vigilant opportunist, the captain saw this raggedy mess of soldiers as a goldmine. Human cargo brought some of the most profitable rates. He sought out the commanding Union Officer in Vicksburg and contracted with him to carry the POWs upstream to Illinois, where they would be let out to find their way home. He would turn this disaster into a pretty profit if he could pull it off.

The lanterns on board the ship were all aglow, seeking to illuminate the darkness for the captain's weary eyes. He was the only one in the wheelhouse. He scanned the river, watching for any obstructions or dangers. He knew too well that a submerged log could easily rip a hole in the hull of his command. It was around one-thirty in the morning and he had not been at ease the entire journey. His severely overburdened craft had performed well so far, but he knew that he would not be able to relax until all the soldiers were off his boat and onto dry land. He stood, eyes red and hands steady on the wheel. He had not slept in at least forty-eight hours, and only for three hours when he did sleep once before.

Mason heard the door open and glanced over his shoulder. It was his first mate. He was a baby-faced young man, courteous, and very by-the-book. "Can I relieve you, sir?" he asked.

"No, no, I'm fine thank you," replied the captain. "Some company would keep me awake though."

"Well I can provide that for you sir," said the mate, stepping into the wheelhouse and closing the door behind him.

"Much obliged. Are the Yanks behaving themselves down there?"

"For the most part, except for them pestering the gator," replied the first mate.

"They'll learn when one of them gets his hand bitten off." The crew of the *Sultana* had caged an alligator on a previous downriver trip. They had kept him on board for several journeys now. The gator acted as a kind of mascot for the crew and provided a novelty for the usual, well-paying guests.

"When we reach Cairo the ship will need some serious cleaning," said the first mate.

"I don't even want to think about it."

"Are you sure you don't want me to take over, sir?"

"Positive."

"You have been awake for two days and nights. I know you're getting tired. Sir it's unhealthy to strain yourself like this."

Captain Mason knew he was right, and secretly he longed for a reprieve.

"You know I am fully capable of steering us safely until you are rested up," said the first mate.

"Well that does sound nice, I won't lie."

"Have a rest sir, you've earned it."

"Thank you son." He relinquished the wheel. "Keep her steady." He exited the wheelhouse. He walked slowly, exhausted. His cabin was just down a short flight of stairs and at the stern. He had to fight his way through the mass of men that clogged the walk. When he finally got to his cabin, Mason shoved the door open and immediately locked it behind him. He took his jacket off and collapsed into his desk chair. They had a long way to go yet.

He needed to unwind before he could get any sleep. He took his pipe out of his desk drawer and packed it with tobacco. He struck a match, lit the pipe, waved the match out, and took a long drag. He exhaled slowly and looked at the brown package lying on his desktop. He hadn't opened it yet and now seemed as good a time as any. He untied the twine and unwrapped the paper. Inside were about forty loose pages penned in familiar handwriting.

> The treachery of this past week shocks even me, how the noblest cause can be twisted to provide a front for such an underhanded seizure of power. My actions, motivated by pure intent, have only proved to provide a catalyst to trade one tyrant for several more, the continent being no better off because of it. How could I have allowed my passion to make me so blind to the true intentions of those who encouraged me to act? The beneficiaries of Lincoln's death will not be the people, but instead a select few who will venture to mobilize the resources of America for their own gain…

As Mason continued to read, a swell of apprehension rose within him and the pupils of his blue-gray eyes dilated. His vision blurred and he took a deep breath and rubbed his eyes. His friend John had entrusted him with the most consequential, dangerous, and damning information the earth. He got up and checked to make sure his cabin door was locked. Could these accusations be true?

He pulled his desk out from the wall and reached behind the left column of drawers. There was a wooden panel fitted neatly in place and could have easily been missed if it weren't for the finger sized hole drilled near the top of it. Behind the panel was an apparatus of his own cunning, used to smuggle information up and down the river for the Confederate cause during the war. He stuck his index finger in the hole and pulled the panel loose to reveal a hidden compartment with a short, fat, steel pipe and a wrench set upright next to it. The pipe was one and a half feet long and eight inches around, sealed off at the bottom end. It had a steel cap on the top that was threaded so that it had to be unscrewed with the wrench. On opposite sides of the cap were two latches that clamped down tight.

The Captain had used this little depository many times during the war, but now that the fighting was over he had hardly expected to use it again for anything other than a place to store cash. The most innovative part of his little safe was that the cap was sealed with rubber rings around the top and bottom of the threads, making it waterproof and airtight. If an accident were to happen, the message would be safe even if he had to struggle to shore with it. As far as he knew, he had the only one of its kind.

He reached down and took the pipe from its hiding place. He undid each latch then unscrewed the cap with the wrench. It was a bit difficult to get started; he always tightened it down hard. There was not anything inside of it at the moment. He took the pages, rolled them slightly, and slid them into the pipe. He screwed the cap back on, tightened it down, and clamped the latches into place. He situated the pipe and the wrench into their hiding place and returned the wooden panel before sliding the desk back against the wall.

The captain sat in his chair, propped his elbow on his thigh, and rubbed his forehead anxiously. He couldn't tell anybody about the diary pages. If he did it might be the most dangerous thing he could ever do. If he proceeded he would have to do it delicately. Did anybody know what John had sent him? He sure hoped not.

BOOM! A massive explosion rocked the ship. Mason fell forward and his face smashed against the edge of the desk and then the floor. He shot up and ran out of his cabin door onto the walk and to the starboard side of the ship. He leaned over the rail and saw that the boiler room had fire pouring from it; an orange inferno shooting through a hole in the side of the *Sultana*. The roaring flames were quickly spreading, igniting the rest of the ship like a floating tinderbox.

Mason heard screams and smelled the pungent stench of burning human hair. Soldiers jumped into the swift water to put out the flames that consumed their tattered uniforms. Most of them were too weak to swim, much less make it to shore. There were dead bodies floating downstream already. Smoke and awful, chaotic cries of desperation permeated the thick night air. Mason tried to hold his breath as he struggled against the panicked soldiers to get to the wheelhouse. He had to do everything he could.

Another huge explosion erupted from the boiler, this one even bigger than the first. It sent Captain Mason hurdling off the ship, thrown like a stick into the rushing water. He landed with a sick splash on the already-lifeless corpse of a young man. It floated facedown with thick black hair waving in the current. He knew that uniform. He turned the body over and when he did he was overcome with grief. It was his first mate. A great, beastly cry emitted from his chest—but it was lost amongst the cruel pandemonium.

The captain fought hard against the water, beating it with his limbs in a frantic effort to stay afloat. His mind raced. What would become of John's secret? Would this monumental injustice stand? He swam as hard as he could but the current was overtaking him. He had a responsibility, he had been entrusted with the truth, he had to stay alive. Mason gasped for breath but got nothing but dirty water. The harder he swam, the farther away from the shore he seemed to get.

Captain J.C. Mason and the secret he carried were lost that night underneath the muddy waters of the Mississippi River.

2

In the eastern Arkansas Delta sat a brown brick house on the edge of a huge loam field planted with soybeans, soil that had been made fertile from centuries of the rising and receding flood waters of the great Mississippi River. There were several tall white oaks in the dirt yard and a recently used fire pit to the side of the house littered with half-melted cans of Michelob Ultra. Concrete steps spotted with dried mud led up to the front door. Nailed to the gable was a corrugated plastic sign that read HIGH COTTON DUCK CLUB in green print with a green duck head below.

The Delta is a place dominated by shimmering rice fields and vast white expanses of cotton. It is a place where the unencumbered wind whips the tall and proud trees into agonizing poses at the borders of the wide fields. There are huge silos there that tower into the sky, their silver exteriors reflecting the hot sun with searing intensity so it often hurt your eyes to look at them on a bright day. Combines the size of small houses stir up dust clouds as they troll up and down the land. This fertile Arkansas plain separates the cities of Memphis and Little Rock—a seemingly endless, flat expanse of agriculture. The Mississippi side of the Delta across the big river is much the same: a wide, hot, dusty flatland that stretches from Memphis south to Vicksburg, bordered on the east side by the muddy, slow-flowing Yazoo and Tallahatchie Rivers. It is where the early blues men would sit on the porches of shotgun houses and play old guitars with their eyes closed, lost in a trance of rough corn liquor and music.

Inside the front door of the mid-20th century ranch house was a living room with a fireplace and above it an old framed print of a black Labrador retriever looking up into an early morning sky over a marsh, scanning patiently for the familiar tint of a flapping wing. There were duck mounts everywhere, old mounts and new mounts, mallard, teal, and wood ducks, their stiff bodies all positioned to make a seemingly synchronized dive bomb on the living room. A black tin sign advertised Jack Daniels, a new flat screen television sat atop a worn entertainment center in the corner, and a caricature of country crooner Conway Twitty silently belted *Hello Darlin'* from its place next to the front door. On one small section of wall beside the empty doorframe that led to the kitchen, Clint Eastwood's wild pistol wielding portrayal growled at the room from a poster for the movie *The Outlaw Josey Wales.*

A tall and confident middle-aged man sat in an imitation leather recliner but did not kick it back to actually recline. Walton Sherman was broad shouldered and muscular in the way a retired navy seal might be. He still lifted weights vigorously but slacked on cardio and was currently half-assing the Atkins Diet, allowing for an extra inch or two around the middle. The jet black wave at the front of his parted hair had a faint sheen of Brylcreem and he had piercing blue eyes underneath thick eyebrows. He was the CEO of his family's business, Union Cotton, one of the largest agri-businesses in the country.

Sherman massaged a worn gold coin between his thumb and forefinger. The man always kept it with him; it was as critical to his daily routine as his wallet. Habitual fondling had made the coin's face shiny and almost rubbed smooth. It was larger than a quarter, more like the size of a silver dollar, one solid troy ounce of precious metal. Occasionally he would flip it up into the air and shuffle it between his fingers like an experienced gambler does with a poker chip. When he was alone he would sometimes find himself gazing at it in contemplative silence.

"Well I've been around and checked all the blinds. The one on the Gator Field needs patching up," he said. "Oughta hit that first and get it knocked out." It was work day at the duck club.

"Sounds like a plan," said Arnold Hackworth, Union Cotton's Chief Financial Officer and a Harvard buddy of Sherman's. He was lounging on the overstuffed couch across the room. His sandy blonde hair was slicked back and his features were sharp and pointy, exaggerated by his lank frame. He had one arm on the armrest and his other across the top of the couch like he was getting ready to cop a feel of an imaginary woman's breast next to him. A Columbia fishing shirt hung from his shoulders. "I got us some new clay slingers the other day, two of them. That way we can do crossing shots."

"I never thought we'd get this high class, damn," joked Sherman. "Speaking of the Gator Field, did you hear how the ole sure-shot senator over here gunned down a duck from the other end of the damn rice field last year?" he asked looking towards an older gray haired man standing in front of the fireplace. He was Thomas Collins, a senior US senator from Tennessee that came from a long line of West Tennessee planters, lawyers, and politicians.

"Uh uh. I ain't heard that one," replied Hackworth.

Senator Collins crossed his arms and grinned expectantly at Sherman. His turkey neck tightened a little, as did his steadily balding brow.

"Well Tom was hunting beside me in the blind and it was bitter cold. We had been sitting there for an hour or so after shooting light and hadn't seen hardly anything. We were huddled around the propane heater and honking on our calls like a couple idiots when this one lonely drake mallard came flying in way over there, way on past the decoy spread. " Sherman pushed his hands away to indicate how far "way over there" was. "Ole Tom pulled up and folded him. It had to be a fifty yard shot." Hackworth nodded in appreciation of such a feat.

Sherman continued, "The dog went out there and got him and we set him on the edge of the blind. We hunted for about two more hours and didn't see a damn thing. Mid-morning we started picking up the decoys and getting ready to leave and Tom grabbed for that one duck and it started flapping its wings and took off. The thing got about half way across the Gator Field before Tom could get his gun back up, but he hit him again and killed it dead. It was one of the funniest things I've ever seen."

The senator chimed in with his deep and authoritative voice. "Yeah it was a big one too. I'm getting it mounted; underneath it's going to say 'The One That Almost Got Away'."

Hackworth chuckled. Sherman wasn't near as country as he made out to be at the duck club. None of them were. In fact they were all used to eating in the finest restaurants, hobnobbing with the social elite, and sleeping in multimillion-dollar homes on their mini-estates in Eads, northeast of Memphis. It was all part of the duck club mystique, an act that they put on to ingratiate themselves with the influential people that they invited out there. Switching on the good-old-boy charm tended to make them seem more trustworthy, or maybe their guests just enjoyed it because it added to the experience, but either way it helped them ink out more deals. Even when it was just the insiders they forgot to break character, or didn't want to. It was fun to get away from the city, slowly drown themselves in expensive whiskey, and pretend that they were just a well-heeled group of country boys.

The Arkansas winters usually harbored droves of migrating water-fowl. The men would hunt during the day, doing their best to make sure that all their guests shot their legal limit of ducks, and they did about half the time. They could have built a ritzy lodge if they would have wanted to, but they preferred the modest brown house. It was anonymous, giving no reason to draw undue attention to the place. At night Sherman would fire up the grill, pass around libations, and turn ESPN on mute. After a good hunt, a big meal, and working up a buzz off of Kentucky's finest exports, most folks were usually more open to persuasion.

Union Cotton owned hundreds of thousands of acres and the five acre plot that the camp house sat on, but they leased the land for the hunting club. The farmer who owned it was the only man whom Sherman had been unable to convince to sell out. He had made numerous offers, each one more outrageous than the previous, but still the farmer wouldn't entertain the slightest idea of selling his land.

A truck could be heard pulling up beside the house, its tires crunching on pebbles in the yard. Sherman's hand closed tight around the gold coin and quickly shoved it into the front pocket of his blue jeans. They heard a truck door open and close, and ten seconds later the farmer's large frame swung into the living room. His name was Ronny Millwood, a tall heavyset man, always jolly and looking for the chance to strike up a conversation. Sherman didn't think Ronny owned a normal pair of pants because he wore Dickies overalls every day of his life. He covered his balding head with an Arkansas Razorbacks trucker cap and kept a sweaty rag in the bib of his overalls to wipe his brow.

"Well hey Ronny!" greeted Collins.

"Hey boys! Y'all gearing up for some greenhead action?"

"Yes sir, you know it," answered the senator. "What's been going on with you, partner?"

"Aw not a whole lot, thought I'd come over and say hey while y'all were all here."

"Having a good year on the farm?" asked Sherman.

"Not bad I reckon. Soybean prices have been pretty good here lately. I think we're gone make it," the big farmer mused with a comfortable smile. "The Mrs. left for Little Rock this morning to see her mama for a couple days, so me and Jr. have got the place to ourselves."

"Always good to have some time away from the better half. Hell, that's why we all come out here," Sherman smiled.

The farmer laughed. "Did I show y'all the stuff I overturned in that big field out there?"

Sherman wanted to jump out of his chair but he hid the intensity of his interest. "No, what kind of stuff you talking 'bout?" he asked coolly.

"Found a lot of old buttons and belt buckles and some different stuff. Looks like it could have been from the Civil War. You know, I'd always heard that the Union Army had a camp around here somewhere."

"That's interesting. Did you find any bullets?" asked Hackworth.

"Naw, no bullets or nothing. After the harvest I plan to go out there with a metal detector and dig around a little. Could be something valuable down there, who knows?"

"Yeah maybe some old outlaw's treasure or something," said Hackworth, widening his eyes sarcastically.

Millwood chuckled and grabbed the straps of his overalls. "Wouldn't that be something? Then I could get me a diesel King Ranch pickup like I always wanted. Y'all going to be doing some work today?"

"Yeah we got to go out and see about patching up some of the blinds," said Sherman as he looked around. He put his hands on the armrests of the recliner and pushed himself up. "Y'all ready? Might as well go ahead and get to it."

"I suppose so," replied Collins.

Hackworth stood up off the couch and they all began to walk towards the back door as Sherman locked the front. "Follow us out the back Ronny." Millwood walked through the kitchen and out of the back door into the yard, followed by Sherman, who locked up behind him. "Ronny have a good day buddy," said Sherman extending his hand. "Gotta get this done so we can enjoy it once the season rolls around."

Millwood shook Sherman's hand. "Got to, y'all don't work too hard."

"We'll try, see ya partner."

The farmer turned and walked past the luxury pickups owned by the members of the High Cotton Duck Club. His head swiveled as he passed Senator Collins' King Ranch Ford half-ton. It was almost like the one he day dreamed about, except he wanted his to have a diesel engine and be Razorback red. His twenty-year-old white single cab truck was parked closest to the road. He opened the door and waved. "See y'all." The men gave an informal wave back and Millwood sat in his sunken driver's seat, started the engine, and pulled away down the straight, dusty road.

Sherman opened the garage door on the front of a white-washed concrete block building behind the house that they called the shop, although there was rarely any work going on in it. He stepped inside and kicked a busted mallard decoy into the corner. A film of dust needed to be cleaned off all of the windows, and cobwebs swept down. There was an old tool cabinet against the back wall and mesh bags of duck decoys piled high beside it. Sherman slid behind the wheel of a four-seater Polaris Ranger and backed into the yard. The senator gathered a few tools and put them into the small plastic bed of the Polaris.

Sherman watched the farmer's truck as it disappeared out of sight. "We're going to have to handle this."

3

Walton Sherman drove his new black pickup along a dirt Arkansas Delta road early the next morning. Thomas Collins rode shotgun and Arnold Hackworth was in the spacious backseat behind him. It was a Sunday. They had the air conditioner turned on full blast and didn't speak a word as George Straight wailed about all his exes being from Texas through the Bose speakers.

They pulled up to a two story farmhouse and parked in the gravel drive beside the detached garage. The house was yellow with a light green door and matching shutters, like a pastel version of the John Deere paint scheme. Sherman stepped out of the truck. His custom cowboy boots hit the ground and a blast of dewy, warming morning air tumbled over him. There was a mixed pack of dogs barking loudly in the backyard. As they walked towards the front door they could see them jumping up and pawing the chain link fence between the garage and the house—labs, blue ticks, and mutts.

The farmhouse was out in the open, surrounded by cotton and soybean fields. Beside it were several large grain silos and a big sheet metal barn that housed Ronny Millwood's tractors. Two tall and stoic oak trees stood alone in the grassy front yard spaced about twenty feet apart. A white swing was suspended from chain on the left end of the wooden porch. The men walked up the steps onto the porch and stood in their jeans beside two motionless rocking chairs bought at the Cracker Barrel on I-40. Sherman rang the doorbell.

"Morning fellas!" said Millwood mildly surprised as he swung open the door already wearing a fresh pair of overalls. "What y'all doing out so early?"

"Morning Ronny!" offered Sherman. "We were thinking about going out there and opening up the back timber hole a little bit, but we need to get your permission first. Would you mind walking down there with us and we can show you the trees we were thinking about cutting?"

"Yeah I can do that. Y'all come on in the house for a minute," said the farmer, and stepped back into the living room.

"Ole Ronny is early to bed, early to rise isn't he?" said Collins as he wiped his boots on the tan welcome mat.

Carpeted stairs led up to the second floor immediately through the door. The living room was eggshell white and a boxy big screen TV sat in the corner. A decade-old family portrait taken for a church directory was on top of the fireplace mantel along with a line of die cast model John Deere tractors. The walls were decorated with needlepoint pictures of angels, Bible verses, and cartoonish farm animals done by Millwood's wife.

"Where's your boy, Ronny?" asked Sherman

"He's upstairs being lazy. Hasn't even woke up yet," responded the farmer.

"Well get him up, and after we get done looking at the timber hole we'll all go down to Kelly's and I'll buy y'all some breakfast."

"It won't be hard to wake him up after you tell him that! Give me just a minute." The farmer went upstairs and roused his son then came back down. "He'll be on down here in a second."

"What grade is he in now?" asked Hackworth.

"Senior this year. Boy is starting tackle on the football team," said Millwood proudly.

"Does he have any college plans?"

"Well you know there's been some smaller schools trying to recruit him. Might play for the Wonder Boys over at Arkansas Tech. I'm not gone tell him what to do, though. If he wants to stay on the farm that'd be alright with me. He can about do the work better'n I can now."

"It will get old living with mama and daddy when he is wanting to bring girls over," said Sherman with a sly grin.

"Yeah," the farmer smiled back. "He can go get him a spot somewhere on the land and build him a house if he wants to. I keep telling him to save his money."

A big teenager came bounding down the stairs barefooted in a pair of gym shorts and a t-shirt. He had a mop of brown hair and swished his bangs aside as he hit the bottom step.

"Morning!" he called as he stepped onto the floor.

"Morning," said Sherman. "You sure did get out of bed quick when you heard we were going to Kelly's."

"You know I wouldn't pass that up," grinned the teenager.

"Well grab your boots son, Mr. Sherman wants us to go look at one of the timber holes with him before we eat," Millwood said.

"Alright," said the young man, and went into the laundry room behind the kitchen.

"Get mine too," his father called after him.

Ronny Jr. came back with two pairs of tall rubber boots and they put them on sitting in the rocking chairs on the porch. "I hope y'all got some of these," Millwood said

"Got 'em in the truck," replied Sherman.

They walked down the porch steps into the yard and went towards the garage. The farmer walked over and patted a baying hound on the head and pulled his keys out of his pocket.

"Y'all just pile in the truck," said Sherman.

"Naw, we'll ride in mine and follow you," Millwood responded.

"I'm serious, no sense in taking two vehicles. I'll bring y'all right back after breakfast."

"You think we can all fit in there?"

"Sure we can, it's only for a minute."

"Alright, I reckon."

They all got into the cab of Sherman's GMC. Ronny Jr. was sandwiched uncomfortably between his dad and Hackworth. Sherman started it up and headed down the road for a half mile. They took a right onto another dirt road which ran along the top of a levee with flooded rice fields glittering on both sides. They continued until the truck came to a stand of hardwood trees. It was eighty acres of oak, beech, and hickory, surrounded on all sides by yet more fields with the closest trees in the distance far across the other side of the crops.

Sherman pulled to the right side and parked; his tires sat on the edge of the levee about three feet above the forest floor below. Collins and Hackworth were on the passenger side and they got out carefully to avoid stumbling down the side of the embankment. Sherman dropped the tailgate and they changed into their tall boots.

Five feet in front of the pickup was a dirt ramp that sloped from the top of the levee down to the leafy ground. It was just barely wide enough to drive a full sized truck down very carefully and beyond it was a rutted and soggy road bed that no reasonable adult should attempt to drive anyway. The men trounced down the ramp into the hardwoods and followed the old road bed deeper into the trees. During duck season this would all be flooded, but right now the water was in the rice fields. Before the season opened, they would pump the water out of the rice fields and into the timber. Now it was relatively dry, with some deep, boot-sucking mud in low spots. The damp leaves muffled their footsteps as they walked.

"Looks like somebody's been down here with a tractor," said Millwood, noting some fresh tire tracks in the mud.

"Yeah we brought one out here yesterday with a loader on the front to pull that old pit blind out of the ground," replied Sherman.

"Y'all get you a new one?"

"Yeah we're gonna go get one."

"That'll be nice."

Hackworth nudged Sherman with his elbow and said, "Ronny I heard you had a nickname that you ain't told us about."

"Uh oh, what's that?" he asked, walking just ahead of them.

"I was getting a biscuit at the Shell station on my way up here and heard some ole gals talking. They said you was quite the ladies' man back in the day."

"Oh yeah?"

"Yeah, I heard they all used to call you "tri-pod". Said you was hung like a Shetland pony."

Ronny Jr. burst with laughter. His father turned around and walked backwards for a few steps. "I don't like to brag but if that's what y'all heard I won't tell you them gals was lying."

"That's what they used to call you huh?" his son giggled.

"That was before me and your mama got married," Millwood said, going along with it.

The group walked on until they came to an opening in the woods roughly twenty yards across and thirty wide, a timber hole. During the winter the ducks would fly overhead and be drawn to it like a magnet. They would careen downwards into the flooded hardwoods and land in the shallow water, searching for food and rest from their migration in the sanctuary of trees that offered protection from predators and shelter from the wind. The ducks would dive under the water, stirring up mud as they looked for acorns hidden under the surface.

The five of them walked into the clearing where a rented tractor waited with a front end loader and a backhoe attachment. Sherman led the way to a small beech tree on the far side. "This one right here ok?" he asked, grabbing a low hanging branch.

"Yeah, I reckon that one would be alright. Y'all didn't have to go rent a tractor. You could have asked me to help," replied Ronny.

"Well we appreciate it but we didn't know what you had going on this weekend. Didn't want to trouble you," said Sherman, and took some pre-cut plastic orange ribbons out of his back pocket. He picked one out, shoved the rest back into his pocket, and took the orange blaze and tied it around the branch just above his eye level.

"Y'all just let me know next time and I'll help you. Save you a little money."

There had always been a good pit blind set back in the timber hole, a steel box in the ground that the hunters could sit in and hide themselves from the scanning eyes of flying waterfowl. It had been fabricated years ago and it sat in the middle of a dirt mound that was four feet higher than the ground around it so that it wouldn't be filled with water when the woods were flooded in winter. Occasionally it leaked, but they always patched it up and it was one of their surest spots for a productive hunt. The blind itself looked like a small, muddy roll-off dumpster sitting on the ground beside the tractor. When Sherman had pulled it out yesterday it left behind a five foot deep hole, then he dug down deeper.

Sherman pointed to a larger tree, this one close to the pit. "How about that one?" he asked

"That one over there?"

"Yeah. Come over here and look at it real quick." They all moved closer.

"I don't think you'd want to cut that one," said Millwood looking up into the tree's branches. "It helps hide you from the ducks when you're sitting in the blind." He walked up onto the dirt mound and looked into the hole. "That thing looks a little deep," he said and grabbed the bill of his hat and twisted it back and forth a few times.

"I don't know if we ought to cut it or not," said Sherman. "I just can't get over how much y'all look alike. A chip right off the old block. You got a little more hair than he does," he said light heartedly, looking at the teenager. "Are you taller than him? Go over and stand next to him. I want to see."

The young man walked towards his father standing on the mound beside the pit. "I can tell you right now he's taller than me," Millwood said as his son approached. The farmer's lips tensed and his eyes narrowed as he glanced into the hole and back at Sherman. Collins was relaxed and Hackworth seemed excited about something. The farmer felt uneasy.

"Y'all stand back to back, I want to see," said Sherman with a toothy smile. "I bet he still can't whip you in a wrestling match."

Millwood relaxed. "Naw, his old daddy will always be able to take him."

"You want to find out?" the teenager quipped. They turned and faced away from each other. Ronny Jr. was taller than his father by about an inch. Sherman looked at Hackworth and snapped his fingers once. It was the signal.

Hackworth whipped out a silenced pistol from behind his back and fired two shots quickly. The farmer's big frame toppled into the gaping pit and hit the bottom with a grotesque thunk. His son writhed on the ground, bleeding from the hole in his temple. Hackworth walked and stood over him and shot again and the teenager stopped moving. He put the pistol on safety and shoved the barrel into the back of his jeans. "Help me throw him in," he said to Sherman.

Sherman grabbed the feet and Hackworth leaned over what was left of the teenager's head to pick up the arms. "Alright, one, two, three," Hackworth said, and they heaved the heavy body into the hole.

Sherman peered over the edge. "Should've sold out," he said coldly, and fished the tractor key out of his pocket.

4

Clifford Carver looked out of his window at the muddy Mississippi River as it flowed south past downtown Memphis. His office was on the ninth floor of the historic Cotton Exchange building at the corner of Union Avenue and Front Street. The old building was at one time the beating heart of the cotton industry in the United States. During the second half of the nineteenth century, and for a good part of the twentieth, the majority of cotton in North America was grown within one hundred miles of this spot. Front Street, located on a low bluff on the riverside, was the most important address in the business and drew the impatient and ambitious with the same gilded temptations as Wall Street. At times the Memphis riverfront would be congested with huge stacks of cotton bales, the white bricks by which speculators sought to build their temples, marking a stark contrast with the coffee-colored current of the river. The Cotton Exchange was where prices were posted and fortunes were made and lost in a matter of minutes under the indifferent auspices of a giant chalkboard.

The advent of computer trading phased out the need for a centralized exchange floor in the city. Cotton bales are no longer piled upon the river bank and the Front Street firms have shut down or retreated into upstairs offices filled with glowing screens. Corn and soybeans are gradually becoming the crops of choice for Delta farmers, but the aura of King Cotton still saunters along the streets of the Memphis business district, evident by faded visual reminders of days gone by. The Cotton Exchange Building has been renovated into a modern workplace and is favored not only because of its amenities, but because it is symbolic, a tangible face for what goes on inside.

Cliff was a commodities trader. He was happy with his success up to this point in his life. Why shouldn't he be? He was thirty-one, made six figures, had an MBA from Vanderbilt, and his student loans were almost paid off. Most people would love to be standing where he was right now, hands in the pockets of a tailored pair of slacks, yet he was restless and that somehow made him feel a little guilty. He was on track to be an influential mover and shaker in his industry, but he did little moving or shaking and instead spent most of his time sitting in a swivel chair staring at numbers on a computer screen. Life wasn't as exciting as he once thought it would be, but at least his ambition had gotten him out of Corinth, Mississippi. He could still be loading sacks of feed at the Alcorn County CO-OP like he did in high school and listening to the farmers bitch about the government and cattle prices. He worked for McIntyre Trading, one of the oldest continuously operating firms in Memphis. Started in 1874 by Zebulon McIntyre, his descendants had steered the business through booms and busts, the Great Depression, and the 2008 Financial Crises, up to now.

The door to his office burst open and Kenneth McIntyre, the last of the McIntyre dynasty, rushed in. "Cliff! Cancel everything you got going on tomorrow! We have some important business to attend to."

"We going to Tunica?" Cliff asked, jokingly referring to the sordid jumble of casinos across the Mississippi state line, knowing in the back of his mind that it wasn't entirely unlikely.

"Oh much more fun than that! There's some prime duck hunting land that's come up for sale across the river and I've got to have it. They're auctioning it off tomorrow and you and I are going to be there."

"You got it. What time does it start?"

"I figure we'll leave here about nine. We're taking the Mustang."

"Hell yeah! You're letting me drive, right?"

"Yeah right," McIntyre scoffed. "Be upstairs at nine."

"Yes sir."

Cliff smiled in amusement as his boss left and closed the door. Kenneth McIntyre was simply Mr. Kenny to him and everybody else who worked at McIntyre Trading. He made it seem fun, and was really the reason that Cliff hadn't acted on the urge to move to Montana, drink a lot of craft beers, and be a fly fishing bum. Mr. Kenny was around sixty and had been married twice, fathering the only two children that he claimed as his own with his first wife—two daughters who wanted nothing to do with the family business. He would regularly pilot his single engine plane to New Orleans with his most recent lady friend and slip in a Viagra between raw oysters and sips of chilled vodka. Cliff knew that Mr. Kenny was scheming already, envisioning an eccentric ducky sanctum.

Cliff was six feet tall, a little stocky, and maintained a lean profile by jogging religiously. His light brown hair was cut into a clean fade. His eyes were green and his nose was straight but not sharp. He didn't take over-the-top measures about his grooming, keeping his morning routine to a concise 15 minutes, and would let his stubble grow on the weekends before he had to shave again on Monday morning. He swore that he would go on vacation and come back with a short beard and not shave it off, but he hadn't worked up the courage to pull that one yet.

His office was on the corner of the building with two windows facing the river and two looking out onto Union Avenue below. It had a row of built-in bookshelves along the left wall that were halfway filled up with important looking volumes of different sizes that he had never read. One shelf displayed an Ole Miss football helmet signed by Archie Manning and his son Eli, both famous quarterbacks from Cliff's undergraduate alma mater. He sat down and opened YouTube on his internet browser and listened to *A Whole Lotta Love* from Led Zeppelin, attempting to pump himself up to process the mundane numbers that changed rapidly on the computer screen.

•••

Mr. Kenny stood up from behind his polished walnut desk in a pair of straight leg jeans and an untucked polo as Cliff entered his spacious office the next morning. It was one floor above Cliff's, and three times as big, with a line of African tribal masks lining the front wall on each side of the door and a wooden Indian standing in the corner. There was a green taxidermy iguana watching over the room inquisitively with yellow glass eyes from atop the left side of the big desk. "You ready to go?" Mr. Kenny asked while patting his pockets to make sure he had his wallet and keys.

"Yeah I'm ready. Let's go."

They took the elevator down to street level and walked into the private parking garage adjacent to the Cotton Exchange Building. Cliff's white four-door Ford pickup was there among the other vehicles, and in the last parking space at the end of the aisle was a gorgeous restored 1967 Mustang fastback. It was dark blue with shadow-style racing stripes and Cliff's face lit up when he saw it. "Yeah baby!"

Cliff opened the passenger side door and slid into the black leather seat, appreciating the clean lines of the classic muscle car. Mr. Kenny turned the ignition and the car roared to life, the engine's growl echoing throughout the ground floor. The garage's heavy steel door rose up automatically when the Mustang got close and they rolled out onto Union Avenue, the sun's slanted morning rays ricocheting off the polished hood. Mr. Kenny pulled his cheap aviator-style sunglasses down from their perch atop his wispy gray crown. They turned left onto Front Street and drove with the current of the river until merging onto the interstate to cross over it.

"How the women treating you, Casanova?"

"I'm pretty ice cold at the moment. Working for you all day really gets in the way of my sex life."

"Aw shucks, I hate that. You should let me be your wingman."

"That's not a bad idea. Weird old guy hits on her then I swoop in to save the day."

"Shit," scoffed Mr. Kenny, "I'd be paying for a hotel room before you got one to agree to let you buy her a drink. You should've learned a few things from me by now."

"Pick out the one that looks like she's just been through a divorce?"

"Nothing wrong with being the rebound. Damn! There's that West Memphis stink again, always hits you like a silent dog fart. You know I've been living here most of my life and I still haven't figured out where that comes from."

It was a distinctive odor, like rotten eggs or worse, and it always awaited interstate travelers just over the Arkansas line. They meandered their way through West Memphis and headed north on a two lane black top. Mr. Kenny had always wanted a son to carry on the McIntyre banner, but his attempts at procreation had not been so inclined. When he had chosen Cliff over a handful of other MBAs he felt like Willy Wonka searching for an unspoiled apprentice to train. Since that time, Cliff had become the closest thing to a real son that Mr. Kenny had, and he determined to groom him to take over McIntyre Trading upon his retirement. Cliff was smart, ambitious, young enough to lead McIntyre into the future, and most importantly he was wrapped a little looser than the average yuppie kid that usually came to him looking for a job. Cliff didn't know it yet, but he was going to get a promotion next month.

"You should start looking for a steady girl. You know the firm encourages children." Mr. Kenny said paired with his best ominous gaze. He was quoting *The Firm*, a movie that every true Memphian has seen multiple times, and at least claims to have read the novel.

Cliff looked at him with a rascally grin. "How would you feel about hooking me up with your younger daughter? We could make you a grand-daddy."

"Hell no. And I say that for your sake not for hers. She'd drive you crazy, all she cares about is drama."

"Uh oh, I don't want no drama mama. You know, I've never been to one of these before."

"What, an auction?"

"Yeah."

"They're fun. They take a while, but they're fun. People watching is the best part. Never know who's going to show up to one of these things."

There was a dirt road intersecting the asphalt up ahead. "That's it," said Mr. Kenny. He slowed and made a clean turn. He drove slowly to try and avoid slinging rocks up onto the Mustang's paint job. They went another two miles before seeing a gaggle of vehicles parked up ahead, all up and down the side of the road in front of a two-story yellow farmhouse. Mr. Kenny pulled up and parked. They got out and he opened up the trunk.

"Oh boy," said Cliff with knowing sarcasm.

"It's nice out here. I'd offer to make you one but you're driving back," Mr. Kenny said as he pulled two red Solo cups out of a half empty plastic sleeve. He produced a can of ginger ale and a bottle of Smirnoff from an Igloo cooler and proceeded to mix himself a drink, transferring the concoction from one cup to the other. He tossed the empty aluminum can into the cooler and closed the trunk. They walked down the road past the other vehicles toward the front yard of the house where a crowd was gathered around a white tent. Mr. Kenny took a drink and smacked his lips easily, "It's gonna be a good day."

Many of the men there were old farmers; there were a few doctors, some overdressed businessmen, middle-aged women who had come for the furniture, and a handful of aloof independently wealthy Delta folk who mostly talked amongst themselves. The auctioneer's tent was set up between two large oak trees in the front yard, and lines of plastic folding chairs spread out in front of it backing up to the porch. Mr. Kenny grabbed a bidding paddle and they took a seat. A well-used recliner was being sold off. The auctioneer's voice ran at a hundred miles per hour in that tireless chatter common to auctioneers. "Do I see fifty dollars? fifty hum-a-nah dollars, hum-a-nah hum-a-nah hum-a-nah. It's a luxurious recliner! Hum-a-nah hum-a-nah. I got fifty to the side! Hum-a-nah."

Cliff leaned over, "Who's selling all this?"

"A widow. Her husband and son disappeared a while back. She doesn't have any other family who wants to take care of the farm. Damn shame," Mr. Kenny answered.

"They disappeared?" Cliff asked skeptically.

"Yeah. She took a trip and when she got back they were gone. Their cars were here, the house was just like she left it, but they were gone. The police haven't been able to find them, or figure out what might have happened to 'em."

"God. That's awful."

"I don't think she's here. Probably couldn't take it. I don't think anybody would blame her."

"That's weird. Farmers are usually the tough and steady type. I wouldn't expect an Arkansas farmer to just up and disappear."

"His eighteen-year-old son, too."

"Man," Cliff shook his head. "There's a lot of weird things going on in the world but it seems to me like there has to be something behind that."

"I think so too, but as to date it remains a cold case."

"Do they have any suspects?"

"No. They don't know if it was murder, or a kidnapping, or what. You would have a hard time kidnapping two big ole boys like that though. They say that they were both about six and a half feet tall."

Cliff sat with a contemplative look and didn't say anything.

"Bad situation," said Mr. Kenny, and exhaled through his nose like he was gently blowing the unpleasant thought from his mind. "Anyway, I expect she will be glad to get my money. I don't think it's going to come cheap."

The auctioneer prattled on until the heavy equipment was sold off, along with Ronny Millwood's white pickup and his son's jacked-up orange Chevy Blazer. The main event was getting close. Mr. Kenny went to make himself another drink and when he came back there was an intermission before they started auctioning the land.

"Kenny! What have you been up to you goofy son of a bitch?!"

"Mac! I still work at the firm a little when I'm not searching for the fountain of youth," Mr. Kenny said as he shook hands and one-arm hugged a man about his age. "Good to see you man. What's been going on with you?"

"You know I sold my practice. I bought some land down in Tunica

County that I've been renting out for the past couple years but my son has been thinking about getting into farming. I came up here to see if they were selling anything that might be useful."

"I hear ya. Mac this is Cliff Carver, my protégé. Mac and I went to high school together at MUS."

Cliff shook hands with the man as he introduced himself. "Mac Marziani. Your boss and I used to have some interesting times together."

"Somehow I don't doubt that a bit. What was he like back then?"

"A nut just like he is now. He used to show up at school in this long black Cadillac from the thirties, looked like Al Capone just pulled into the parking lot."

"It was my grandfather's old car. You talk about chick magnet," smiled Mr. Kenny.

The old classmates reminisced for another ten minutes and parted ways with a "Call me and we'll go grab dinner," from Mr. Kenny. There were others at the auction that he knew, too. Most of the time people who had several million dollars to slap down on farmland ran in the same social circles. Mr. Kenny was feeling pretty good halfway through his second drink, one that he had made a little stronger than the first. He exchanged pleasantries and his customary retort to handshakes, saying, "Shakes are for strangers, move on in for the real thing," and then proceeded to bear hug unsuspecting acquaintances.

Finally the auctioneer called out, "This is it folks, the moment many of you have been waiting for. We are going to sell the land with all the buildings including the beautiful home behind you. We will not subdivide. This is for the entirety of the real estate fee simple. Out of one thousand one hundred and forty acres total, we have seven hundred and sixty acres of cleared, highly productive loam farmland, some of the most fertile soil in the whole world that will pay dividends every year. There are also three hundred and eighty acres of valuable hardwood timber spread throughout the property. We will start the bidding at six million dollars. Do I see it?"

A man close to the tent raised his paddle. "I've got six!" rang out the auctioneer. "Do I see six and a quarter? Six and a quarter?" Another paddle shot up in the middle of the crowd. "Right over here! Do I have six and a half?" The bidding continued on that way until they had reached eleven million dollars and there were only two men left bidding. Mr. Kenny had yet to raise his paddle. One of them was a fellow that Cliff had shaken hands with earlier and Mr. Kenny had ambushed with a brotherly embrace. The other man Cliff hadn't noticed before, and he looked a little nervous. He had a brown comb-over and wore a plain light blue button-down tucked into his khaki pants. He was clean shaven and appeared to be of average height sitting in the plastic chair at the end of Cliff's row. His jaw was tense and it looked like he was consciously focused on controlling his breathing. At first glance he was just another anonymous stiff, but his shirt sleeves were rolled up to his elbow and on the inside of his right forearm was a tattoo of a scorpion.

"Eleven one hundred! Can I get eleven one hundred?" The stranger raised his paddle hesitantly. "To the gentleman on the right! Back to you sir! Eleven point two?" the auctioneer shouted and pointed at the other bidder who thought about it for a moment and painfully held up his paddle. "How about eleven and a third?" The stranger shook his head. "Eleven million two hundred fifty thousand? Eleven two fifty? Eleven two fifty?" The stranger raised his paddle. "Eleven two fifty on the books! Eleven and a third! Eleven and a third, sir?" The other bidder didn't move and had a look of heart attack level frustration upon his face. "Going once..." began the auctioneer.

"Fifteen million dollars!" Mr. Kenny cut him off and hoisted his paddle high with a shit-eating grin spread wide across his face.

"Wowweee! Fifteen? Sold! Sold to that man for fifteen million dollars!" the ecstatic auctioneer yelled as he pointed to Mr. Kenny and slammed down his gavel. He walked from behind the podium and stood at the edge of the stage as a buzzed Mr. Kenny strutted up to him. "Congratulations sir! That was quite a surprise ending!"

"I have a flair for excitement, what can I say?"

"You want to do some paperwork?"

"Absolutely."

Cliff stood in the yard and noticed the stranger walk to a late model sedan and get in without saying a word or looking at anybody. He closed the car door, put on a pair of sunglasses, and fumbled with a pack of cigarettes that had been sitting in the cup holder. He lit one and cracked the window before driving off. He went away from West Memphis, away from anything really. Cliff puzzled over it for a moment but let it go as Marziani approached him.

"Typical Kenny style."

Cliff laughed and nodded, "That's him."

"I can tell you one thing."

"What?"

"There isn't anybody on the planet who will have more fun with this place than he will."

"No doubt."

•••

That night the stranger's car pulled into a run-down roadside motel. A rusted metal rail ran around the second floor walkway. It had a sign out front that read "PAY BY THE HOUR." There were only three other cars in the parking lot, none of which looked to be under twenty years old. He read the room numbers as he crept along. 131…132…133. He pulled into a space close to room 133 and got out. He took one last shaky drag from his Camel, dropped it, and ground it out on the parking lot with the ball of his foot. The stranger walked forward, swallowed nervously, and knocked on the door.

"Yes?" came a voice from inside the room.

"I'm looking for Mr. Phillips."

"Mr. Phillips?"

"Yes. Sam C. Phillips, the record producer."

The door swung open and the stranger walked inside, then it closed quickly behind him. The room was dingy and illuminated only by a small lamp on the bedside table. The decrepit double bed wore a stained comforter that had cigarette burns, and the sight of it made the stranger's skin crawl. There was a small table to his left beside drawn beige curtains and a buzzing A/C unit. The uncomfortable wooden chairs upholstered in light green were torn, with dirty whitish fluff protruding from their back rests. Walton Sherman sat at ease in one of them, with his back to the wall, wearing a gray suit. He fondled the gold coin in his right hand. Senator Collins locked the door and said, "Take a seat." The stranger sat in the open chair by the table with his back facing the bed.

"So how'd it go?" Sherman asked.

"Not as anticipated."

Collins, standing a few feet away, crossed his arms and drilled a hole into the stranger with his dictatorial glare.

"What the fuck does that mean?" grilled Sherman.

"Well sir, I got into a price war with another man and it got over eleven million dollars. I bid last and thought I had it locked up…" he shook his head apologetically. "The auctioneer started to count down and a guy at the other end of the row shouted out fifteen." He stopped and took a shallow breath. "I was shocked. I just kind of sat there for a second and by the time my mind started working again the gavel had gone down and that was it."

"Fuck! You fucking piece of shit!" Sherman ejected and pounded his fists on the table, squeezing the coin tightly. The stranger jerked back as if Sherman was going to come at him.

"I'm sorry. I wasn't expecting that to happen."

"You could have yelled out sixteen million! Twenty! Hell, whatever it took!" Sherman lowered his voice and shook his index finger at the stranger aggressively. "We hire you to do one simple thing and you can't deliver. This is fucking unbelievable."

"It was hardly my fault. I had remembered what you said about not looking too eager. My instructions were not to draw any suspicion."

"You screwed up big time," said Collins.

"Did you at least get the name of the guy who bought it?" asked Sherman.

"Name was McIntyre, Kenny McIntyre."

"Shit. I know who he is. One of the biggest weirdos in Memphis."

"He didn't bid at all until he threw up his paddle at the end."

"Of course he didn't."

The stranger tried his best to sit still and look tough but on the inside his nerves were melting. "We had an agreement. I still get paid."

"Like throwing ten thousand dollars up a wild hog's ass," Sherman snarled. "Nobody who was at that auction is to ever catch a glimpse of you again. Go bury your head in the sand somewhere until I tell you otherwise. You understand?"

"Completely. Where is my money?"

Sherman pulled a stack of one hundred dollar bills held together with a white paper band out of his jacket. He let the money flop down on the table. The stranger picked it up and flipped through it, taking a mental inventory. Sherman scoffed and glowered at the stranger, insulted by his nerve.

"Thank you." The stranger rolled the stack of cash and put it into his front pocket.

"What, you didn't think it was all there?" Sherman opened the left side of his jacket to reveal a shoulder holster with a gleaming stainless steel pistol tucked into it. He stared at the stranger for a few long seconds and then closed his jacket and sat back. He propped his elbows on the armrests and looked the stranger in the eye—unblinking, unflinching. "You need to get the fuck out of here and drive until you get to the other side of Arkansas," he finally said. "You better not test me on that."

"Yes sir." The stranger stood up, thankful to be leaving. He walked past the senator, who followed him with his glare, unlocked the door, and left the motel room.

"This ain't good, Tom," Sherman said as he heard the sedan pull away.

The senator uncrossed his arms. "Walt look, the most important thing is that nobody knows anything anymore. Nobody has a clue about that farmer, either. I doubt very seriously this McIntyre guy has any other motivations than trying to have some fun and shoot some ducks."

Sherman began to turn the coin over in his hand. "We can't afford to take that chance. That land isn't going to be his very long anyway."

5

Brevard Pope was a genteel relic of a slower and more feudal time, though that time had past a generation before he came along. His family had owned and lived on the same plantation outside of Brownsville, Tennessee since before Brownsville was a town. While the Pope family's attitudes had become more progressive along with the Episcopal Church, Brevard's deep, unhurried drawl and his anachronistic mannerisms would have fit seamlessly into the Mississippi State Senate during the 1920s. He had kind azure blue eyes that seemed to recognize the hidden potential that one secretly hopes to apprehend within themselves and a laugh that reverberated directly from the center of his broad chest. He always smelled of Clubman aftershave and a recently smoked cigarillo, and was given to anoint men under forty with the moniker "sport." After a successful and highly lucrative career as a geologist in the oil and gas industries, Pope led a semi-retired lifestyle meticulously restoring his family's plantation home and commuting into Memphis to teach history at Rhodes College, a small liberal arts institution with a beautiful collegiate gothic campus.

He relaxed in a modernly styled leather chair with his white bucks on a tanned cowhide rug in Mr. Kenny's office. Mr. Kenny sat in a matching chair across the driftwood coffee table with a rocks glass of Maker's Mark. It was late in the afternoon and they had just finished going over Pope's account with McIntyre Trading, a relationship that had been going on since Pope moved back to Tennessee. Brevard Pope was not only a client, he had become one of Mr. Kenny's closest friends. They had been baking boozed under the Destin sun and braving the cold on the hunt for trophy mallards together for the past decade. Whenever Pope came to McIntyre Trading, he was always strategically scheduled to show up around four so that he and Mr. Kenny could enjoy a libation or two.

"I bought a new pair of waders last week. I'm ready to go kill some ducks as soon as y'all get that place ready," said Pope.

"Oh it's gonna be awesome," said Mr. Kenny. "I got a guy doing some work on it right now. He's ripping out the carpet and putting some fake hardwood down. I bought some new appliances for the kitchen and a sarcophagus of a deep freeze. I'm going to unleash my inner Emeril out there."

"Good. You're a lot better cook than you used to be," Pope grinned.

"Every bad meal is a learning experience, Brevard. We are going to have some boisterous times out there buddy."

"Absolutely. I'll have to contribute to the liquor cabinet. Did they ever find out what happened to that farmer and his boy?"

"No, the whole thing is real strange. There was nothing gone out of that house. Not a thing. Unless they set out on foot with nothing but the clothes on their backs, they had to be with somebody."

"There wasn't any blood or any sign of an altercation?"

"Nowhere." Mr. Kenny shook his head in disbelief. "It couldn't have been random. Maybe the farmer had some enemies, I don't know, but I don't think that somebody just happened by. You have to know where you're going to even find that place."

"Or maybe his son had gotten tangled up in the wrong crowd."

"Could be. Whatever happened, they didn't leave a trace."

"They just... vanished?" asked Pope, waving his glass of bourbon.

"That seems to be the consensus. I still don't think the police have any idea."

"Things like that go unsolved a lot more often than we'd like to believe. Sort of puts some bad voodoo on that place, don't you think?"

"Nah," Mr. Kenny quipped. "It'll be alright. I've got a lot of good karma built up. I feel so awful for the wife though. I saw her one time. There were some guys from their church helping her move some stuff out. She was trying not to cry. She looked pitiful."

"Hmmm," Pope grunted sympathetically. He placed his glass on the side table and looked down. "That's sad."

"Yeah…" Mr. Kenny took a sip of his drink and looked towards the window. "I didn't know what to say to her. She looked at me almost like I was stealing something from her. I just told her I was sorry."

"Well you can't help that. I'll have to bring my dog, he loves going to new places. He'll have a time sniffing it out."

"Oh yeah he's always invited. You know, I found out after I bought that place that Union Cotton had been leasing it out as a hunting club. They were none too happy to hear that I wouldn't be leasing it to them anymore."

"Really?" Pope asked, intrigued. "Who'd you talk with over there?"

"A fella named Walton Sherman, he owns Union Cotton. He called me and just about begged to buy the land from me. Told me to name my price. He said they'd been hunting it for fifty years."

"Boy, sounds like you could have made him a deal," laughed Pope.

"He'll be ok. I don't imagine the CEO of Union Cotton will have a hard time finding another place to hunt."

"I'd say he shouldn't. They've got their pick of choice spots. It seems like they own about half of the Delta. Every time I look up they're buying more land."

"Wonder why they were leasing that place then?" Mr. Kenny asked speculatively.

"Shoot, who knows. Probably because they can. They got more money than Fort Knox. It's fairly close to town isn't it?"

"Not too far, it's only about 30 minutes from where we're sitting."

"That's probably why," said Pope.

"I imagine so. You ever met that guy? Sherman?"

"No, never have."

"He's a stout dude to be fifty-something years old. Kind of has that politician air about him, you know," Mr. Kenny said, making nebulous gestures with his hands. "Seems like a nice enough guy though."

"Maybe you should invite him to come hunt with us. Wouldn't be a bad guy to know," suggested Pope.

Mr. Kenny sucked in through his teeth. "I don't know, might just be a little insulting."

"Yeah, maybe that's not such a good idea... Well, I better be going." Pope stood up and finagled his arms into a sand-colored cotton sport coat.

"Alright man, I'll see you again soon." Mr. Kenny stood up and followed him to the door. "Drive safe."

"I will, don't get into any trouble without me," Pope jived.

"I already got you beat," Mr. Kenny laughed, and closed the door.

He took his glass of whiskey and sat behind his desk. He swiveled around and watched the sun begin to touch the Arkansas horizon across the river. Everyone else was gone for the day so he could indulge himself in a guilty pleasure. He opened his top drawer and reached for an old, worn wooden duck call that had accompanied him on many hunts. MallardTone was inscribed across its chestnut body. He held the call to his lips and began to chatter and quack unapologetically, anticipating the season to come.

•••

Cliff lived in a craftsman style bungalow in Midtown Memphis close to Rhodes College. Overton Park and the Memphis Zoo were to his south and it was a cheap taxi ride back home from the bars in the Cooper-Young district, a couple blocks of hangouts frequented by hip locals and college students. The house was a fixer upper and Cliff had spent many weekends sanding off old paint, ripping up carpet, replacing sheetrock, and making trips to Home Depot. He was proud of his efforts and of the lightly used refrigerator that he had recently gotten cheap off a buddy for helping him move. It was just after nine p.m. after a long day at work as he sat in a lawn chair at the trusty coffee table that had followed him around since college under the soon-to-be-replaced light fixture at the front of the kitchen. He relaxed, perusing the latest issue of Fast Company magazine and munching on a takeout BBQ sandwich. He was contemplatively regretting his decision to order hot sauce instead of mild when his smartphone rang.

"Hello?" he answered, mouth half-full of BBQ and white bread.

"Yes, is this Clifford Carver?" the male voice sounded grave and apprehensive.

Cliff swallowed the bite. "Speaking."

"Mr. Carver, you work at McIntyre Trading with a Mr. Kenneth McIntyre, correct?"

"Yes I do," he answered, puzzled.

"I'm Officer Marlon Jackson with the Memphis Police Department. I'm afraid I have some bad news to share and you were found to be his closest contact."

Cliff's brow ruffled. "What happened?"

"There's been an accident. Mr. McIntyre is no longer with us."

Cliff's heart stopped beating as the phone slid off his ear. That's not happening. Mr. Kenny was a like a father to him, a friend closer than most of his family. Mr. Kenny was bulletproof, he couldn't die. He had seen something in Cliff, taught him to be more than he was, shown him how to succeed outside the defined realms of academia. Mr. Kenny really was the most important person in his life, Cliff realized. He began to hyperventilate and felt a blunt, excruciating whelp form in the center of his chest. His head buzzed. This isn't happening.

"Mr. Carver? Mr. Carver are you still with me?" the phone squawked.

Cliff came back to reality and put the phone to his ear. "Yes, yes I'm here. What kind of accident?"

"He was in a car wreck. He wrapped his vehicle around an oak tree on the side of Poplar Avenue. Can you come meet us?"

Cliff fought to calm himself. "Absolutely. Where are you?"

"We are close to the Belle Meade neighborhood in front of Second Presbyterian Church. Please be careful and obey the speed limit getting here."

"Yes sir. I'll be there as soon as I can." He fought back tears but couldn't help the droplets that slid down his red cheeks. Mr. Kenny had made more of an impact on his life than anybody. He was the best mentor that Cliff could've ever hoped to find. He quickly went outside and started his truck. Mr. Kenny lived in Belle Meade with the other old money people. He was almost home. Cliff backed out of the driveway, more vigilant than ever before. As he drove the emotions seethed within him, his chest rose and fell painfully and he beat on the steering wheel a few times.

He saw the flashing lights from the fire truck when he got close. Mr. Kenny's silver Mercedes had centered an oak tree and the engine was smashed backwards into the cabin, where it crushed his boss. The front of the car was hardly distinguishable and the side was a mangled array of metal where the firemen had cut out Mr. Kenny's body with the Jaws of Life. There were two squad cars and an ambulance parked in the front lot of the Second Presbyterian Church. Cliff pulled into the lot and parked behind one of the police cars. An African-American police officer stopped him before he could get out of the truck. Cliff rolled his window down and spoke to the man. "I'm Clifford Carver. I talked with Officer Marlon Jackson on the phone."

"I'm officer Jackson. You can step out of the vehicle Mr. Carver," he said and stepped back.

Cliff got out of the truck and felt weighed down, a wave of helpless anguish rushing over him. Everything seemed to happen in slow motion. "Where is he?" Cliff asked.

"He's inside the ambulance already. Don't go over there. You want to remember him as he was, not how he is now."

Cliff gazed at the twisted wreck in disbelief, unwilling to accept it. The flashing lights bounced off the side of the church. "Mr. Kenny was always a good driver. I just... I just don't understand."

"Was Mr. McIntyre a drinker?" asked the officer.

"He was on occasion, yes."

"Might this have been an alcohol-related incident?"

"I don't know, I wouldn't think so. He was always careful. When I was around him he seemed to know his limits."

"Judging by how far he swerved off the road, this kind of thing makes us believe that he might've passed out behind the wheel. But, and we don't have conclusive evidence, we also think that his vehicle could have been tampered with."

"What?" Cliff snapped his gaze from the wreck and looked the officer in the eye, unable to comprehend the idea.

"After inspecting the vehicle, our team believes that it's likely Mr. McIntyre experienced brake failure."

"But that car was only a year old," Cliff protested.

"I know. Did Mr. McIntyre have anyone who would have been motivated to hurt him?"

Cliff struggled to absorb the question. "No! Everyone loved Mr. Kenny. He had tons of friends."

He couldn't believe that anyone would have a reason to murder Mr. Kenny. He had never heard him talk badly about anyone. He was wealthy and came from an enviable background, but so did other people. He never talked down to anybody, it didn't matter who they were. Mr. Kenny always seemed to carry some kind of rogue optimism around on his shoulders.

"I realize that this is a difficult question to open up to, but I need you to think very seriously about it. Your answer could make a big difference."

Cliff took a deep breath and searched his brain, laboring to come up with anything. He looked back at the wreck that a group of firemen were working to peel off the tree. He thought hard, but for the life of him he couldn't pick out any suspects. He looked back at the officer and said, "I honestly can't think of anybody right now."

Officer Jackson handed Cliff a card. "This is my number. Please call if something comes to mind later. The hardest thing about this, Mr. Carver, is that it's nearly impossible to get any identifying evidence off a wreck as torn up as this one. If there was any foul play involved, the culprits may never be found. I'm afraid we may not ever be able to understand why this happened."

•••

Three days later Cliff stood in Mr. Kenny's office. It would be his now if he wanted it, but he didn't, at least not yet, not like this. It had been specified in the will. Cliff was shocked by it, and so were Mr. Kenny's daughters who had hoped for a quick sale of the firm and an ecstatic trip to the bank, but McIntyre Trading was now his. Mr. Kenny had never told him, and he supposed that he understood why, but he was altogether unprepared and floored when he found out. Cliff felt overwhelmed at the responsibility that had been suddenly thrust upon him. In the will Mr. Kenny had called him his adopted son, and he couldn't express how much Mr. Kenny meant to him, but he had to try at the funeral that afternoon.

He looked around the room, meditatively examining the relics of a life well experienced. There were the tribal masks on the wall that he had procured on an African excursion to climb Mt. Kilimanjaro, the wooden Indian salvaged from a forlorn general store, and the pensive iguana, whose origins were a mystery. He picked up a picture from the bookshelf. It was a young Mr. Kenny, in what he must have thought was a rather romantic flying outfit, standing next to a bi-plane with a pretty girl leaning on him. Cliff smiled understandingly and nodded his head.

Cliff moved over to the desk and opened the top drawer. A big smile spread across his face because knew he would find it there. Cliff picked it up and held it. MallardTone. He ran his thumb up and down the side of the well-used call. Mr. Kenny used to love to stay late in the office so he could watch the sun go down over the river. He would sit up there in his big chair, watch the last orange glow of the day disappear over Arkansas, and blow that damn duck call. An idea suddenly struck him and Cliff placed the call in his pocket.

•••

At the funeral Cliff stood at the podium and tried not to tear up as he unfolded his speech. Mr. Kenny's closed casket was below him at the altar in the front of the packed room. He looked out at the crowd and recognized his coworkers, Mr. Kenny's small family, Brevard Pope, Mac Marziani, and others among Mr. Kenny's countless friends. He smoothed the letter out on the wood and took a deep breath.

"Kenneth McIntyre was a person that we all admired very much. His zeal for life was inextinguishable and inspires us to approach our own lives with the same sense of wonderment. He was a man who always managed to leave others with a smile on their face and renewed spirit in their hearts. He pursued his passions and encouraged us to cultivate and realize our own dreams. To all of us at McIntyre Trading, he taught that business is not simply about business, but about the business of living a full life. He was a wonderful mentor to me and a great friend to us all, and he will be greatly missed." Cliff paused for a moment. "I will be stepping into the role of President of McIntyre Trading. I promise to all of the friends of our firm and to all of our associates that I will do my best to become more like Mr. Kenny."

Cliff felt his eyes begin to water, and a tear dripped onto his suit. He folded the letter and walked down. A hymn played as Cliff and others carried the casket down the aisle and to the awaiting hearse. At Elmwood Cemetery they lowered the casket into the vault under a granite obelisk that was engraved MCINTYRE. Cliff watched it slowly go down. He squatted next to the hole as the casket got close to the bottom. When its descent stopped he wiped his eyes, reached into his pocket, pulled out the old MallardTone duck call and tossed it in.

6

On Monday of the next week Cliff met with Brevard Pope. They met in Cliff's old office; he couldn't find it within himself to move upstairs just yet. They didn't talk about Pope's account, or about the market, but instead reminisced about their friend and searched to salve the wounds from his passing. They sat in front of the desk in the two client chairs facing one another. Pope held his right knee as he spoke, his right foot propped across his left knee.

"I remember Kenny used to try to get me to go flying with him," said Pope. "I'll admit I was a little scared. I even get nervous about flying commercial, much less a little single prop with Kenny driving the thing. He used to have one of those little racing planes with two seats, a driver's seat in the front and one behind it, like a World War II fighter plane. It had 'The Star Destroyer' painted on the side of it." Pope laughed. "He finally talked me into getting in that thing with him. It was fun for about thirty minutes. We flew around and looked at the city and flew down the river a little ways. Then he yelled into the headset, 'You ready to have some fun?' and before I could answer he sent that plane into a nose dive, pulled back up and did a loop, and then went straight into a barrel roll. I yelled so loud. I was never so glad to get back on the ground in my life." Pope chuckled robustly and Cliff laughed along with him.

"Oh man," began Cliff, "I remember this one time some people from New York flew down here. They wanted to have a meeting with us about some kind of new fund they were trying to get together. They put on a good show, everyone one of them acting like they were some kind of big shot, some pretty ostentatious looking folks. It felt like we were having a meeting with the mafia. There was this one woman with them who was just the rudest person I have ever met in my whole life. You could tell that it wasn't her idea to come down here and that she thought we were a bunch of hicks. She looked like she was drugged out on pills the whole time. So they gave us their pitch and we were getting ready to go eat lunch right? We walked out the door of the building to go down the street to the Rendezvous because they were in Memphis, and said they wanted some Memphis BBQ," Cliff said as if beleaguered him. "She was walking behind Mr. Kenny and me and we overheard her say that she was surprised we were wearing shoes."

Pope's face formed into a look of shock and Cliff raised his eyebrows, grinned wittingly, and continued. "Mr. Kenny stopped and turned around and asked, 'Excuse me, would you say that again?' and she went, 'Oh I didn't say anything.' Mr. Kenny said, 'I heard exactly what you said. Y'all all listen to me closely because I don't want to repeat myself. We don't care for any of you a bit and this meeting is now over. Please don't come back to our office.' Then he goes, 'Come on, Cliff,' and we started walking away, and that woman started screaming, right on the sidewalk on Union Avenue. 'You rednecks aren't walking out on us! We won't tolerate this from some down south hicks! You aren't walking out on us!' He turned around and went, 'Yes we are, you nasty bitch. Fuck y'all.' Then he flipped them all a bird and we went and ate a pizza."

Cliff started a bout of unhinged laughter and Pope joined him, and when they were through they both felt a bit of release. Cliff sat back and brushed his hair to the side with his hand as his laughter died down. "I'm going to Chez Philippe tonight," he said with a grin that bordered on cavalier.

"Oh really? She must be a very special lady."

"I wish that were the case. I'm meeting with somebody from Union Cotton. They asked me about buying that farmland the firm owns. I'm going to see what they'll give me for it. The price has to be right, though."

Pope leaned back, brought his hands together in his lap, and furrowed his brow tentatively. "I don't know about that, sport. You're talking about the land Kenny got at that auction, right?"

"Yeah, what's wrong?"

"Didn't he tell you?"

"Tell me what?"

"They already tried to buy it. Union Cotton called Kenny and said they'd buy it if he'd sell it to them and he wouldn't."

"Oh," Cliff looked down a moment, perplexed. "I didn't know."

"I wouldn't rush into this if I were you. Kenny wouldn't have wanted you to sell it. He wanted that place to be around to enjoy, for you enjoy," implored Pope. "Why are they so eager to get their hands on what you have?"

"Well I already told 'em I'd be there. I don't have to sell it. A free dinner at Chez Philippe can't be a bad thing."

Pope looked at him soberly and shook his head. "Don't sell it, especially not so soon. It would be disrespectful."

Cliff could tell that Pope was very serious. "OK I won't. I'll just go have dinner."

"Good." Pope turned his head and looked out the window in thought. "This deal sounds a little fishy to me. Something's not right."

"I'll be careful. What do you think is going on?"

"Ah…" Pope breathed out. "I can't exactly put my finger on it but I was the last person to see Kenny before he died. I don't think that he was that drunk. We had a drink together in his office and I went home about seven-thirty. He might have kept drinking after I left…" Pope took a breath and sighed. He brought his hands apart and held them in air in front of himself. "I've been around Kenny a whole lot and I've never seen him try to drive if he was that bad off. I don't think he would've gotten behind the wheel of a car if was so drunk that he was going to pass out and run into a tree," he said with finality, and let his hands rest.

The police officer's speculation of foul play lingered in Cliff's mind but he kept it to himself. "I'll be fine. I'll let you know how it goes," he said, trying to offer some reassurance.

"OK, please do." Pope stood up to leave and Cliff followed him to the door.

"Thanks for coming by, Mr. Pope."

"Goodbye Cliff, call me," he said, and looked Cliff in the eye as he shook his hand. Pope turned and walked out the door. Cliff shut it behind him and walked thoughtfully back to his desk. He sat down, opened his internet browser, and typed "Union Cotton" into the search bar. The company website came up, a Wikipedia page, a farm news website with a recent article, and a consumer action group protesting the company along with other large agricultural corporations. Cliff clicked on the Union Cotton website.

"Union Cotton – Pioneering Sustainable Solutions for the Future" is what the headline read across the top of the homepage. There was a landscape photograph of a perfectly white cotton field being picked by a new combine below the letters, with an early morning sun casting golden light that ideally complimented the color of the field. Cliff scrolled down. Below that was a picture of a gaunt but smiling African man in a wide brimmed hat holding out a handful of furry cotton seeds, and a link that said "Our Seed Programs Help Raise Growers' Incomes in Sub-Saharan Africa." There was another picture of an empowered-looking young adult with a "Career Opportunities" button above her head. He scrolled back to the top and clicked "About Us."

There was a black-and-white photograph of several middle-aged white men with their pants held up past their navels by suspenders standing around a 1940s tractor. "Union Cotton is an American family-owned business, three generations strong," began the paragraph. A handsome face that Cliff thought he recognized smiled halfway down the page. He sat back and studied the picture for a moment. Why did he seem familiar? The caption below read, "Walton Sherman – Chief Executive Officer."

7

Cliff, in a slate gray suit and freshly shaven, followed the maître d' up the stairs to a table close the far left corner of the posh dining room. He was meeting Lee Dalton, a representative for Union Cotton, with whom he planned on enjoying a cordial dinner and then politely refuting whatever offer that he proposed. The restaurant was busy, but not completely full, and several empty tables buffered the corner for privacy. The white-clothed table was set with two menus, sparkling silverware, and full water glasses. Opposite him with her back to the wall sat a stunning woman in a form-fitting black dress. She had naturally wavy copper-blonde hair, chestnut eyes, and a wide shapely mouth complementing her jawline. Cliff was curious, looking her over thoughtfully as he sat down.

"You must be Mr. Carver," said the woman, extending a well-formed hand across the table.

"I am," he said taking her hand gently, "and you must be Lee Dalton?"

"Yes. It's a pleasure to meet you Clifford Carver."

"Likewise. Call me Cliff." He took a sip of water as he studied her. This was pleasantly unexpected.

"You look a little surprised," she said.

"Delighted. I was led to believe that Lee Dalton was a man."

"Oh, it's L-E-I-G-H, and I was under the impression that I was having dinner with a big red dog."

Cliff laughed quietly, "My mother wanted to name me after someone important." Leigh smiled, one corner of her lips turned up higher than the other, and her perfectly symmetrical nose crinkled minutely, almost imperceptibly, but Cliff noticed and he was enticed. "What do you do, Ms. Dalton?"

"I'm a buyer mostly. I help Union Cotton manage their assets."

"It's harder to turn down an offer from a pretty face." She looked him up and down with amiably tightened lips and Cliff wasn't sure if she felt complimented or if he had questioned her aptitude.

"Something like that. Officially I'm the Acquisitions Manager for the Mid-South Region."

"Sounds important," he said. She wore an easily confident countenance and gave the impression that she didn't feel the need to defend her intelligence in order to hang with the boys. There was something innate about her that told him no special effort had gone into looking so strikingly beautiful, as if elegance were her natural state of equilibrium. Cliff couldn't deny that he was intrigued by this woman, but he told himself that she still couldn't convince him to sell.

"Do you have a title?" she asked

"Yes I do, but I'm not very comfortable with it yet. My late boss, Kenneth McIntyre, was killed in a car accident recently. I've taken over his position."

"I'm so sorry," she said, leaning forward.

"I was very close to him."

"I can't imagine what you're going through. I wish there was something that I could say."

"I appreciate it. There isn't anything you need to say. I can't help but notice that you don't sound like you're from around here," said Cliff, noting her clear, librarian like pronunciation and absence of long vowels.

She sat back, her slender frame straight, gracious, and tempting underneath the black dress. "I'm not. I grew up in Seattle," she said proudly.

"How'd you end up in Memphis? Seattle seems like a much more interesting place."

"They made me a good offer and I didn't mind a change of scenery, so here I am. To someone from the Pacific Northwest, the South is an interesting place."

"Not much in the way of natural scenery around here. It's flat as a table. It's not a bad place to live though, I guess."

"No I like it, but it is very different from Seattle."

"I've never been but I'll take your word for it," said Cliff with a self-depreciating smirk. "No one knows the faults of the South as well as a Southerner. What's it like up there?"

"Oh," she looked up and shook her head gently, her hair lightly brushing the back of her neck. "There's like a million sushi places," she laughed.

"They've got some good sushi down here, too. Get you a catfish and tomato roll."

Leigh snickered. Cliff picked up the menu. "What do you think looks good?" he asked. They discussed it for a few minutes and ordered. They decided on sharing a bottle of pinot noir and the waiter poured some of the crimson inebriant into two long-stem glasses before setting the bottle on the table between them.

"I bet you get to do this a lot," Cliff said.

"Do what a lot?"

"Wine and dine."

"That is a part of it, yes," she answered warily.

"I'm sure that being beautiful doesn't hurt your job performance."

"Thank you, and no it doesn't," she said with a perceptive smile. "Am I going to have to turn you down before the night is over?"

"I don't know, I can't speak to your level of restraint," returned Cliff, quite proud of himself.

Leigh emitted a burst of laughter and said, "For you I'll be about as restrained as an old nun."

"You'd be surprised at the nuns I've had."

"I think I'd be surprised at more than that," she grinned, and shifted in her seat before raising her wine glass to her lips.

They made small talk while they ate their meal and then the waiter cleaned the table. Cliff picked up the wine bottle and gestured questioningly at Leigh. She nodded and he poured more into her glass before doing the same to his own.

"Now, Ms. Dalton, what is your company's proposal?" he asked.

"We are prepared to offer you thirty million dollars for your agricultural holdings in Arkansas," she said staidly.

What the hell? Cliff tried not to let his surprise show. That was double what Mr. Kenny had paid, and he paid too much to start with. What were they doing out there before? Running prostitutes in and out of the camp house? Hosting dog fights in the dry timber hole? Shit, that much money would probably keep most people from asking questions.

"Thirty million dollars?" he queried with some unintended cynicism.

"Yes, that's correct."

"I'm curious… since Union Cotton owns so much land already, and could buy more land anywhere they wanted, why are y'all so interested in our thousand acres in Arkansas?"

"We are trying to enrich our portfolio in the United States. As I'm sure you know, the world population is exploding and agriculture is the most essential industry to the vitality of the human race. We have very fertile and very valuable farmland right here in the U.S.—land that is fast becoming the world's most precious asset. With a stable government and high technological advantages, we believe that the United States is the best place for us to invest."

Leigh spat the answer out fast and smooth, like she had memorized it out of a playbook. Cliff knew that he wasn't the first one who had been delivered that line. That was some smooth dancing.

"Why do you want our property in particular?" he asked.

"We are currently working on securing tracts all across the South and Midwest and yours would be a very nice one to have, not mention that it's relatively close to Memphis and could have future development potential."

Geez, she was painting some broad strokes. If she wouldn't give him a straight answer there was no way he would consider the offer; besides, he had already promised that he wouldn't sell. But thirty million dollars? He'd be an idiot not to take that. Did they know something that he didn't? He wasn't sure, all he knew is that he had already made up his mind.

"Well that is an extremely tempting offer, but I'll need some more time to think it over. I need to get through taking care of everything in regards to all the changes that have been taking place here recently. I'm sure you understand."

Leigh was obviously disappointed but replied, "I do. I wish I could have met Mr. McIntyre. He sounds like a very likeable man."

"He was a very likeable man... he would've probably tried to hit on you though."

She smiled. "It's on the table. Just let me know."

"Thank you."

God she was good-looking. He wished that she was sitting across the table because of him and not because she had to for work. She's doing her job, he reminded himself, just like you're doing yours. Don't mix business and romance, that's not good protocol. *But how can you pass up this opportunity?* he asked himself. She's sexy, smart, and she looks like she's about your age. Come on man... Mr. Kenny would tell you to go for it.

"Leigh, I noticed that you aren't wearing a ring. Would you consider having another drink with me?"

She investigated his face for a few moments, trying to sort out his intent. "I wouldn't be opposed to it at all," she finally said.

"What do you like? If dinner is on Union Cotton, these are on me."

"I'll have a cosmo."

"I'm going to have a manhattan." They gazed at each other silently for a few moments. "What do you enjoy the most about your day?" he asked.

Leigh batted her eyes and smiled a little seductively. "All the interesting people I get to meet, of course."

Cliff laughed. "That's a good line."

"A little flattery never hurt anyone," she said assuredly.

"I suppose you're used to getting flattered by men."

"Oh I don't know about that." She put her elbows on the tabletop, placed one hand on top of the other and leaned forward, her eye's fixed upon Cliff's. "Why? Were you going to attempt to flatter me?"

"I wouldn't dream of it," he said calmly.

"Oh really?" she quipped, narrowing her eyelids.

"Flattery connotes an exaggeration of the truth. I don't have to lie to tell you that you are incredibly beautiful," he said warmly.

She blushed as if she didn't expect it, looked down horizontally at the table, and glanced back up at him, very pleased with his answer. "That's the truth, huh?"

"Every word."

"I appreciate a man who doesn't lie." Her slender ivory neck curved as she turned her head. "So what do you like the most about your day?"

"All the interesting people I get to meet, of course," Cliff teased, bringing his hand up and back down, drawing a line in the air from her head to her waist.

She rolled her eyes and shook her head. She should have seen that one coming. "I mean about your job."

"I do my best not to discuss work past six." The waiter walked by and Cliff ordered their drinks.

"That's a good rule," she said as the waiter left.

"It makes for more interesting conversation. Do you like to read?"

"I do." She looked at him attentively, hoping for a connection. "What's your favorite book?"

"My favorite is *A Confederacy of Dunces* by John Kennedy Toole."

She gasped excitedly. "No way! I love that book! I read it right after I moved here."

"It's wonderfully absurd. I never get tired of the adventures of Ignatius Reilly."

She laughed. "I know! It's hysterical! I love the part when he tries to rescue Harlot O'Hara from the Night of Joy. And his muscatel loving mother? The characters are so well developed."

"Oh, they are. I love how he describes Gus Levy and his wife that's always harping on him. You can almost believe that the whole story actually happened. You know, I often feel like Ignatius Reilly," he said in a jokingly cerebral tone.

"You have violent gastro-intestinal problems, yell at the screen when you go to movies, and still live with your mom?" she smiled and giggled at her own accusation. She brushed her bangs out of her face with an easy swipe of her index finger.

"No, well at least my mother doesn't mind. The world according to Ignatius Reilly makes perfect sense to Ignatius Reilly, even when everybody around him doesn't get it. In the land of the blind, the one eyed man is king. At least he feels that way to himself while others think that he's the blind one."

She smiled thoughtfully, subtly entertained. "I think that most people who think for themselves feel that way at times. I have. We all live in our own strange little worlds."

"It would be an awful thing to be unfortunately normal. You want me to let you in on one of my eccentricities?"

"Please do."

His face showed mysterious danger, as if he were about to reveal the location of a stolen Rembrandt. He spoke slowly and deliberately. "I have a large collection of outlandish socks." His eyebrows jumped and his bottom lip was stoic after he imparted this earth shaking knowledge.

"What?" she laughed and looked at him like she thought he was an intriguing goofball.

"It's true. I always wear superbly unusual socks." He held his leg out and pulled his slacks up to reveal bright red and blue polka dotted socks that went halfway up his calf.

"My. You live dangerously."

"I enjoy a life on the edge." He swiveled his leg back under the table as the waiter set their drinks down.

"Nice socks," commented the waiter.

"Thank you, I only adorn my feet with the finest stockings," he said looking at Leigh provocatively. She held back an amused snicker. Cliff tasted his manhattan. "That's pretty good."

The waiter was smiling at them both quizzically. "Wonderful, I'm... glad you'll enjoy it," he offered and walked away.

"So tell me about yourself. What's your favorite book?" Cliff asked.

"Oh there are so many, but my favorite is probably *Midnight in the Garden of Good and Evil*. There are lots of great characters in that one, too. And to think that it's based on a true story? Have you read it?"

"Oh yes. It's a classic."

"I used to think that everybody in the South was like that book," she admitted a little repentantly.

"Well we don't all drink like fish and shoot each other in moments of passion, but there are a few of those old society people still around. Some of my clients are like that. You know, 'Everybody comes to my Christmas parties,'" he quoted in his most affected drawl.

Leigh laughed. "That's great! Any of them have voodoo séances in the old cemetery?"

"Oh I'm sure there are some. I wouldn't be brave enough to find out. There is a place in the south part of town people call Voodoo Village. It's all fenced in. You drive by and there are all kinds of strange-looking symbols everywhere, crosses, and statues of the Virgin Mary with the paint peeling off. I've heard stories of witch doctors and orgies and all kinds of weird stuff. Legend has it that if you drive by at midnight your car will shut off and they'll drag you out and turn you into a zombie."

"Ooooooooo. Spooky. I bet you can run into a Lady Chablis or two on Beale Street."

Cliff chuckled, "Oh yeah. I am positive you can. You can find Elvis down there, too. The real one. He won't be singing. He's the overweight old fella with pork chop side burns that hits on the waitresses at Silky's. I know he gets frustrated that he can't tell them he's the real Elvis."

An entertained, reactive stream of air blew from her nostrils and she laughed. "What else do you do in your spare time?" she inquired, honestly eager to find out.

He took a tactful sip of his cocktail. "I like to put on my alligator boots, turn Burning Love up real loud, and play air guitar in my birthday suit," he said, doing his best Don Draper impersonation.

She burst with laughter despite trying to keep it down, causing other restaurant guests to turn and look at them. "What a coincidence," she said in a quiet, high-voiced response from her lungs only being half filled with air.

"What? You have alligator boots too?" he said with a straight face.

"I like to do the same thing to Tina Turner songs."

"What chemistry! That's incredible. I'll think we'll just have to sing a duet later."

"You think so?"

"I really do. I don't think *Proud Mary* could ever sound so good."

"Only if we can do *Hot Legs* by Rod Stewart after that."

"Absolutely," he drew out. "I feel like you just fell from heaven. I bet you like to sing in the shower, too."

"Every morning."

"What kind of angel is this?" Cliff blew a soft stream of air from his lips like he was trying to cool off his tongue. "I might even have to break out the extra special sensual sounds of Teddy Pendergrass," he grinned.

"It's like you have a window into thoughts," she smiled. "Am I going to be impressed with your singing? I hope you can hang with my golden pipes."

"Oh." Cliff feigned offense. "They don't call me The Alabaster Nightingale for nothing."

She laughed. "I can't wait to find out. The soulful songbird and the velveteen vixen," she said smiling, touching her hair and tilting her head slightly with a cheerful glance to the ceiling.

The waiter walked by. "Excuse me, could we get our checks?" Cliff asked.

"You know in Seattle I used to stay up all night and listen to jazz, drink cheap champagne, and smoke long Audrey Hepburn cigarettes."

"That sounds scintillating."

"It is. It liberates your mind and heightens your senses," she said in a way that was intended to be mysteriously enticing.

"I think I'd enjoy that after our concert."

"Good."

They paid their tickets and walked outside of the Peabody Hotel, the grand old dame who keeps the city's most intimate secrets locked inside her walls. Cliff hailed a taxi as they stood beside the Duck Walk Hall of Fame, bronze duck prints imbedded in the sidewalk that are emblazoned with the names of influential Memphians. The King of Rock and Roll, Elvis Presley, is of course, among them. The prints reflect the popularity of the Peabody's live mallards that swim daily in the fountain in the center of the hotel's illustrious lobby.

The taxi door closed and the pair glided excitedly through the door of Cliff's house. The living room was decorated with large black-and-white prints of photographs of rock stars offstage. Robert Plant held his clenched fists out victoriously from the balcony of a trashed hotel room, Keith Richards smoked insolently on a couch, Ronnie Van Zant held a shotgun over the arms of his rocking chair, and Waylon Jennings pointed at the camera with Uncle Sam-like conviction. Cliff turned on his speakers and started The Rolling Stone's *Honkytonk Woman*.

Leigh kicked her high heels off, held her arms out, and Cliff gladly took her hands. He swung her to one side, then the other, and spun her around underneath his hand. She came back to him and pushed off, reeling out and extending her free arm wide. She reeled back into him and Cliff caught her and let his arms absorb her momentum and held her low. Her back arched, her blonde hair swung down, and she held her chin up as Cliff wafted and then kissed her neck. She grinned sensually as Cliff pulled her up and they continued to dance, their hips getting closer with each chorus.

The distinctive pumping piano of the intro to Burning Love filled the living room. Leigh smiled with an anticipatory gaze. Cliff pulled her body into his, ran his nose up the inside of her left breast, followed her neckline, and breathed her scent deeply as he raked through her hair. She breathed out onto him and pushed her hands underneath his dinner jacket, gripping his torso tightly with the tips of her fingers. They swayed back and forth, Cliff unzipped the back of her dress, and she wiggled in assistance as he pulled it off of her. She lifted her feet out and Cliff shimmied down, running his cheek down her body and skimming over her tight black lingerie. She exhaled heavily onto his neck and pushed his jacket backwards, prompting him to take it off. He did as she gripped his belt and pulled him into her. Her lips worked their way up Cliff's neck until they found his mouth, and the night only improved from there.

8

It had been a long day at work. The past week had been a whirlwind at the office dealing with everybody and trying to figure out what the hell he was supposed to do now. Cliff could tell that some of the older associates were a little miffed at the way things had gone down and were less than pleased to be working for somebody who they saw as a thirty-something-year-old kid. Trying to strike the right balance of friendliness, Mr. Kenny-like unorthodoxy, and authoritative confidence was hard.

He ate alone in a booth in the corner of Soul Fish Café in Cooper-Young. He was worn out and reflected on the day while he sipped a craft brew and munched fried catfish. It was Friday night, he might call Leigh and see what she had going on this weekend. That would provide some stress relief. He didn't think that he had ever gotten it on like they did, Lord have mercy. I bet she'd want to go out and listen to some music with me, he thought to himself.

An attractive young woman of Asian heritage slipped into the bench seat across from him. She was wearing a professional looking skirt suit and at first glance Cliff thought that she might be fresh out of law school. Her straight black hair fell halfway to her shoulders and she wore a no-nonsense smile. "Would you like some company?" she asked.

Cliff was a little startled but he wasn't going to say no. "Uh… sure."

"My name is Zoey Nguyen. I know who you are."

Cliff cleared his throat in surprise. "What?"

"You're Clifford Carver, you work at McIntyre Trading. Handsome, successful, a very eligible bachelor."

What was going on? Cliff really didn't know what to say to this stranger. "Thanks… What can I do for you?"

"You have in your possession a piece of land that Union Cotton wants very much to buy. You aren't considering selling it to them are you?"

Cliff's brow furrowed and he was perplexed. How did she know about that? "It hasn't really been my most important priority lately."

She looked back at him soberly. "We would like for you not to sell it to them, but keep lines of communication open between yourself and Union Cotton."

"And who is we? Who are you?" he asked guardedly.

"I'm with the Federal Bureau of Investigation."

Cliff's eyes refocused and his mouth opened slightly. He looked at her quizzically, a little frightened and unsure if he had done something wrong.

"Don't act surprised. Be natural," she said easily. "We have an ongoing interest in Union Cotton and its owner Walton Sherman. We would very much like your help with this investigation."

"Have I done something illegal?" he asked, feeling very anxious.

"No, you haven't done anything of criminal interest to the bureau."

He felt slightly relieved, but only slightly. "I really don't know how much of a help I can be."

"You're in a perfect position to help us a great deal. Your new role at McIntyre Trading allows you a certain degree of freedom and mobility. It also gives you access to people that others might have a hard time meeting with, and it allows us to create convincing alibis for you talking to these people. You are an ideal candidate."

"You want me to be a spy?" he asked skeptically.

"We like to say informant," she bluntly returned.

"Are you really in the FBI? How do I know you're telling the truth?"

"I guess you don't, do you?" she said with some aggravation in her voice. "Do you expect me to whip out a badge?"

He was unsure, and he was very uncomfortable. This can't be real, right? "What have they done?" he asked.

"As you know, Union Cotton has been aggressively buying up land all over the Delta regions of Arkansas, Mississippi, Louisiana, and Tennessee. All the money for these acquisitions comes in from offshore and it's hard to trace. We suspect that Sherman is skimming money off the top of Union Cotton's revenues and hiding it through a web of shell corporations, and then wiring that money back to purchase land. Last year we had the IRS do an audit on them but it came back clean. The bottom line is, we aren't sure where the money is coming from and we would love nothing more than to be able to convict Sherman of accounting fraud and tax evasion."

Cliff felt an impulse to remove himself from this situation as quickly as possible. "Look, uh…Zoey. I have a lot on my plate right now. I really don't think that I should get involved with this."

She stared back him sternly. "You would be doing a great service for your country and for yourself. Think of your own industry. McIntyre Trading deals in agricultural commodities; Union Cotton influences the supply of some of those commodities in a big way. Don't you want to make sure that everybody is playing by the rules?"

"We'll play by the rules and have a profitable business. If someone else wants to hang themselves with shady dealings they can go right ahead. Ma'am, I'm very sorry but I really don't want to have any part of this."

A waitress walked by and Cliff held his hand up. "Excuse me, can I get a check please?" The waitress nodded that she heard him and walked on. He wasn't even halfway done with his plate.

"Cliff, this is a case that could potentially be worth millions, if not billions of dollars," Zoey implored. "If you cooperate with us I'm sure the government will be…" She paused, searching for the right word. "Appreciative."

Cliff was beginning to feel threatened and a defensive ball of anger was building inside of him. "Zoey, I have plenty of money," he retorted. "My responsibilities are with the firm and our employees. I won't help you." He shifted his weight and dug into his back pocket for his wallet. He opened it and began to count out enough cash to cover his bill and then some.

"Leigh Dalton could end up in jail as an accessory to fraud. Do you want that happen?" Zoey whispered forcefully. "You looked like you were really enjoying her company the other night."

Cliff had the money in his hand and was about to lay it on the table but he stopped immediately. "How do you know about that? Have you been following me?" he demanded in a hushed tone.

"We've been following her," Zoey corrected.

"What?"

"She is usually the only face from Union Cotton that a seller sees during these deals. We've been keeping our eye on her now for a while."

Cliff paused introspectively. He laid his closed wallet on his thigh. He felt lied to, deceived, and it hurt. He had wanted to call her, but now he felt bad about the idea of maybe having some feelings for her. "Is she being investigated? Does she know about the money?"

Zoey crimped her lips and narrowed her eyes smartly; surely he didn't just ask that. "They're all being investigated Cliff. We aren't scratching anybody off the list."

"Does she usually sleep with everybody she tries to buy land from?"

Zoey smiled and shook her head. "No. She's usually very efficient. You should see some of the people that she has to deal with."

That somehow didn't make him feel any better. He took a deep breath through his nose and set the two twenty dollar bills on the table top. He put his wallet back into his pocket. "I'm not doing this. I'm sorry." He stood up.

"You do realize that if you tell her about this conversation, or anybody for that matter, you can be prosecuted. I would think very hard about turning us down," Zoey cautioned from the booth.

"I'll forget this even happened. I just want to go to work and be left alone. I won't be doing any business with Union Cotton. Thanks for the warning." Cliff walked out of the restaurant and could feel Zoey's eyes on the back of his head.

He got into his truck, feeling a little edgy. He breathed shallowly as he drove and turned on the radio to try and distract himself. His eyes darted back and forth, watching the road and other vehicles apprehensively. He was all of a sudden very conscious of his driving. As he turned into his driveway, his cell phone buzzed. He cut the truck off and walked onto his porch, afraid that it was a text message from Leigh. He nervously drew the phone out of his pocket, trying to think of how he would reply. The message read "Zoey Nguyen", and underneath was her contact information. Shit! How the hell did she know his phone number?

He shoved the phone back into his pocket, fumbled with his keys and hurriedly opened the front door. He walked quickly into the kitchen, got a tumbler glass from the cabinet, filled it with tap water, and gulped it down. He refilled the glass and held it as he stood there. His heart was beating too fast. He set the glass down and put both hands on the countertop, leaning into them, head down. "Just chill. You've got to chill out. Take it easy. Think about something fun," he told himself. He tried, but he couldn't get the text message out of his mind. She must've been the real deal.

Did he smell something? He sniffed twice. It wasn't a good smell. Now that he was aware of it, it seemed to be everywhere. He sniffed again. Sulphur? It smelled sort of like some of the fertilizer he used sling. Oh shit, he thought, I've got a natural gas leak somewhere. Where's the most likely place for a leak? It's an electric stove… check the water heater and turn the pilot light off!

Cliff bolted to the door of his laundry room and opened it. He flipped the light switch and knelt down to look under the water heater. Thank God the pilot light was out. He felt some momentary relief. Geez, the smell was overwhelming in here. He looked hard at the copper pipes but it was too dark underneath to really see anything without a flashlight. He stood back up and checked behind the water heater's tank. His eyes followed the gas line coming out of the wall and… Are you fucking kidding me? Someone had sawed a section out of the pipe with a hacksaw. He wiggled his way toward it and looked closer.

A dim flashing red light caught his eye from behind the dryer. He looked. There was something duct taped to the wall. It was the size of a Snickers bar, and six red numbers on the front read 00:00:17. They changed. 00:00:16. 00:00:15. "Shit!" Cliff screamed and ran as hard as he could. He burst through the front door, bounded off of the porch over the shrubs, and sprinted down the street.

Cliff felt the explosion just as much as he heard it. He turned around and the house had been blown apart. The walls and beams that were still up were quickly being consumed by violent orange flames. Thick black smoke tunneled into the sky. He heaved in and out desperately, wide eyed, and his nerves shrieked with panic-induced adrenaline. No. No. No. No. No...... ...... No! No! No! No! No! He loved that house, had poured his heart into it, had spent so much time fixing it up. All his pictures, all his stuff, everything! It was all gone. He was afraid to go near his truck to try to save it, as the fire roared only a few feet away from its grill. Oh my god. What had just happened? Cliff looked around. Neighbors were appearing on porches up and down the street. What could he do? What he could do? He desperately tried to think. He began walking up the street, his mind bouncing back and forth between conclusions.

He remembered that the police officer had speculated about foul play being responsible for Mr. Kenny's wreck. It was only after he'd gotten involved with that land in Arkansas that it had happened. Union Cotton had already tried to buy it from Mr. Kenny. The FBI. Thirty million dollars? There was no doubt in his mind now that Mr. Kenny was murdered.

What could he do? What could he do? He didn't feel safe here. Zoey. He pulled his phone out of his pocket, clicked on her number, and pressed send.

"Cliff. Have you changed your mind?" she answered.

"Come get me. Right now," he demanded.

"Sure," she said with concern. "I'm on the way. Where are you?"

"I'll be at the Snowden Avenue entrance to Rhodes College in five minutes."

"I'm coming. I'm in a black Tacoma with blacked out windows. Are you OK?"

"Someone just tried to kill me."

"What happened!?"

"Somebody filled my house with natural gas and stuck a bomb in my laundry room," he breathed heavily. "Good thing I smelled it right after I walked in or I'd be dead."

"I'll be there as quick as I can."

He didn't really know what it was, but something told him to run. Cliff shoved the phone back into his pocket and ran down the street towards the college.

•••

Cliff was distraught and still not feeling very calm as he and Zoey walked into the FBI offices. They walked down the hall into an open room where half of the twenty transparent cubicles were occupied by people engrossed in computer work. "This is our geek squad," joked Zoey. "These folks are dangerous." She led Cliff down the aisle and turned into a cubicle plastered with Batman memorabilia, where a middle-aged Hispanic man was leaning back in his office chair as he typed. She placed her hand on his shoulder. "What's up, Marvin?"

He looked up casually. "Hey Zoey. Saving the world one key stroke at a time," he said, then looked back down.

"Marvin, this is Cliff Carver, our newest team member," Zoey said.

Marvin swiveled around. "Oh really? Hey brother, Marvin Cervantes. I feel like I already know you." He stuck his hand out without standing up.

Cliff shook his hand warily. "You do?"

"Oh yeah. I know your life story already, man. Glad you said yes. I was afraid that you wouldn't."

Cliff looked at Zoey weirdly and back at Marvin. "Marvin, someone just tried to kill me. I'm here for protection more than anything."

"Oooh. That's no good. I'm sorry to hear about that. So... you're in, right?" he asked flippantly.

Cliff still didn't feel good about it, but this was undoubtedly real and an attempt had just been made on his life. Maybe this could get him some answers about Mr. Kenny. He was about to bite the bullet in spite of himself. "Yeah. Yeah I'm in."

"Sweet," said Marvin, and swiveled back around.

"Got anything new Marv?" asked Zoey.

"I've been tracing these wire transfers all over the place. This thing is more tangled than an Alabama family tree. There is this name that keeps coming up, though—The Gayoso Fund. Any idea what that might be?"

Zoey shook her head, "Google it."

Marvin clicked another window open on his desktop and swiftly hit a few keys. "Manuel Gayoso de Lemos," he read. "Governor of Spanish Louisiana, 1797 to 1799."

"Huh," shrugged Zoey. "I don't know. Keep looking." She turned to Cliff. "You feel alright?"

"I guess. Better than I was feeling."

She smiled, "You'll be fine." She slapped him on the arm. "You stick with us and pretty soon you'll be one badass smooth operator. You can crash here tonight. Go get you a shower. Come on, I'll show you." She began to lead him out of the room.

"So what exactly do you want me to do?" he asked

"Wear a wire and go to meetings." She looked him up and down. "We'll have to get your measurements here in a minute. You need a tux. You're coming with me to Washington."

9

Cliff and Zoey sat in the back of a FedEx truck, at least that's what it looked like to everybody walking down the sidewalk that night in Washington, D.C. A burly, bearded driver named Chuck was in the front and he and Zoey both wore the purple and black uniform of a FedEx delivery person. Cliff was looking pretty dapper in his tailored tuxedo. The inside of the truck had been outfitted as a rolling field office. Three computer screens lined the wall above Cliff's head. There was a scanner and a printer beside him, among other gadgets that Zoey had told him not to touch.

"Alright, you ready?" asked Zoey.

"Yep. Ready as I can be," Cliff replied.

"Anybody behind us?" she asked Chuck.

"You're clear," he responded.

"It's party time. Go shake what your mama gave ya." She rolled up the back door of the truck, Cliff stepped out into the street, and she quickly rolled it down again. He turned a corner, walked a few blocks, turned another, and could see the White House illuminated in a stately glow on the other side of Lafayette Square. He turned one more time beside St. John's Episcopal Church, its tall steeple piercing the velvety night sky like a needle, and then made his way up 16th Street.

Cliff nodded to the doorman as he tried to look casual strolling into the lobby of the St. Regis hotel. It was luxurious and had a decorum that gave the hotel an old-world feel. He was attending a political hand grab there; the invitation in his pocket read "The American Environmental

Awareness Gala." *Man*, he thought as he looked around, *this place makes The Peabody look like a Holiday Inn.* He felt nervous. He needed to warm up a little. He found a bar and ordered a Maker's Mark on the rocks, then people-watched for around half an hour.

He found that he was enjoying himself inspecting the party guests that shuffled through the door. There were bulbous balding men with their few remaining strands of hair locked in place like concrete. Other men had hair that was too shapely to be natural, like silver George Jetsons in Armani suits. Some of the women had plastic smiles, and dresses that covered up everything, leading Cliff to speculate that they were doughy from political lives of frustration and inebriation. Many of the guests had apparently already served themselves before they arrived. "Yeah, you should hear Bill Clinton talk about it, man," Cliff overheard. "Fella is a student of kama sutra. He told me how to do some things that blew her fucking mind." There were plenty of gaudy furs and exorbitantly rotund watches to go around. Cliff thought the best ones, though, were the spray-on tanned election hopefuls who had sand-blasted themselves Oompa Loompa orange for their TV spots.

He finished his drink and followed one snide looking couple onto the Astor Terrace where the gala was being held, noting the unnaturally stiff gait with which they both walked. He scanned the crowd and didn't see who he was looking for yet. He made half a lap before being accosted by a social climbing law student who must've thought that Cliff was someone important.

"Hello sir! How you doing? Randall Price Kettering," he said with nasally intonation, thrusting a well moisturized hand at Cliff.

"Hello sport. Beauregard Cummerbund, Attorney General of Louisiana," he said in his most convincing southern lawyer's protraction. "How do you feel about this bill that everyone is so excited about?" This was great. Cliff always thought that he would've made a good southern attorney, especially coming out of the environs of the Ole Miss Law School.

"Well sir, I think that it would just be a wonderful thing for our country and set a responsible precedent for future legislation. The main issues addressed by this bill have been plaguing efficient natural resource usage for the past half-century. The way I see it, if concerned Americans fail to act drastically now, it may be too late to salvage any hope of a more biotic North American ecosystem."

Cliff smiled and placed his hand on the young man's shoulder firmly. "Well I say son, I do believe that you might be the only person at this soirée who read past the cover page."

"Thank you, sir. You come across as a very astute gentleman." The young man smiled as widely as he could. Cliff kept a straight face, holding back his laughter. He longed to offer this kid a bogus summer job but he restrained himself.

"Well I appreciate that, Mr. Kettering. Judging by your verbal acumen, I should reason to say that you can put together a mighty fine summation."

"Yes sir, I have been known to author some real doozies for moot court."

"Now tell me, which law school was fortunate enough to have you as their student?"

"Emory sir, Emory University," he replied swiftly.

"Oh Emory, that's a lovely old campus down there. How did you get interested in the legal profession?"

"Well sir, I just have such a robust passion for justice. It's every citizen's right to have skilled legal representation. The virtue of due process is so incredibly exciting."

Cliff almost let a chuckle burst forth. This was amazing. He was like Robin off the old Batman TV show, the one with Adam West in it. Cliff halfway expected him to stick his fists into his hips, puff his chest out, and go "Holy Smokes, Batman!"

"Well son, don't ever lose your enthusiasm for the justice system. As for me, I'm going to go do shots with Ruth Bader Ginsburg," Cliff winked. "Don't ever confuse morality with legality," he smiled suggestively, and walked away.

Walton Sherman was sipping champagne and talking to a short, portly, and pink faced man across the way. Cliff sauntered towards him, waved, and said loudly, "Mr. Sherman! I had no idea you would be here!"

Sherman was taken aback by Cliff's sudden introduction and it showed in his face. He might've been surprised to see him alive. Sherman knew who he was—that little shit that Kenny McIntyre wagged along everywhere. His lips twisted into an ugly scowl before quickly correcting themselves. Sherman fabricated some composure and said, "Cliff, I had no idea you'd be here, either. How are you doing?"

"Doing explicitly sensational, sir. How about yourself?"

"Just fine."

"I imagine you'll be doing a lot better after this bill gets passed, huh?" Cliff said, and nudged Sherman enthusiastically with his elbow.

"Ha," Sherman came up with an uneasy laugh. "Well we are doing pretty good as it is Cliff."

"Hi, Cliff Carver," he said sticking his hand out to the piggish gentleman on his right.

"Marty O'Donnell," he replied.

"Cliff, Marty is a United States Congressman from Oregon," offered Sherman.

"Oh wow. What do you think about this bill?"

"Well you know, I think that it's important to have a clean environment. I really think that it will be good for farmers. Having a clean environment is especially important for people who work outside all day," said the congressman.

Boy, this guy was sharp. Cliff shot Sherman a shrewd glance. "Well that's an admirable sentiment," he smiled. "Tell me more, I'm here to learn."

"Yeah aaaahhhh..... clean air, clean water, clean dirt—who can't get behind that, right?" He belched an uncertain chuckle.

"Cliff, I didn't know that you were so interested in conservation," said Sherman.

"Yeah, I smell what you're stepping in. I haven't been to D.C. in a while either, so I seized this opportunity to come up here. Some people I work with are concerned about the ins and outs of this bill, and I figure that it's my job to stay current on these things."

Sherman stared back at him suspiciously. "Did you get an invitation?"

"Well obviously. I wouldn't be here if I didn't. I'm on the mailing list, man," he grinned confidently.

"From what I understand," began O'Donnell, "this new legislation will provide support to both agriculture and wildlife enthusiasts. It will really go a long way towards protecting our natural heritage. I'm voting for it."

"Great," said Cliff. "It sounds like you have some ties to agriculture."

"Well not directly, but my brother-in-law provides capital to growers in the burgeoning medical marijuana industry."

"Oh" said Cliff, surprised, but trying not to act like it. "Well alright then."

"Where is home for you Cliff?" asked O'Donnell.

"Memphis, the same as Mr. Sherman. I almost wasn't able to make it up here. This past week almost killed me," he said lightheartedly with a glance at Sherman. Sherman's cool façade didn't break, but his eyes were cold and hardened. "Please excuse, gentleman. Enjoy the evening," he said and walked to the bar.

A string quartet in the corner played the Spring section of Vivaldi's *Four Seasons*. Cliff recognized the tune. *How appropriate*, he thought to himself. He got a beer from the bar and surveyed the party scene. Senator Thomas Collins was huddled around a tall cocktail table with two other men. Cliff identified him immediately but wasn't sure if Collins would recognize him. He walked up nonchalantly and they politely gave him their attention. He couldn't tell if Collins knew who he was or not, just that he didn't seem disappointed that he wasn't dead.

"Hi guys, Cliff Carver. Mind If I join you?"

"Not at all," said Collins, in high spirits and already a little lit. Cliff extended his hand for a round of introductory handshakes. "Thomas Collins," offered the senator amiably.

Next to him was a younger, thinner man and Cliff knew who he was too. Truman De Luca, downtown Memphis's former foremost ambulance chaser-turned-congressman. At one time he had a giant billboard on Poplar Avenue that read "In a Wreck? Want a Check?" Cliff didn't vote for him.

"Truman De Luca," he said as they shook hands. "Pleased to meet you."

"Pleased to meet you as well," Cliff returned in his most sincere voice.

The last man introduced himself pompously as "Howell Jennings Davidson Ellsworth the Sixth".

Damn if this wasn't the waspiest dude he'd ever met in his life, enhanced by his tie that had some kind of crest dotted all over it. "Good to know you," Cliff returned.

"Mr. Carver, what do you do and what brings you here?" asked the senator.

"I'm in agricultural commodities. I try to stay abreast of the latest legislation that could affect the industry."

"Superb," ejected Ellsworth the Sixth.

"I think you'll find that *The American Waterfowl Habitat and Mississippi River Alluvial Plain Preservation Act* will be very beneficial throughout the supply chain," gloated Collins.

"Senator Collins and Congressman De Luca co-authored it you know," Ellsworth the Sixth informed Cliff.

"Really? Tell me some more about it. I need to do a little more studying on it myself before I can decide to support it or not," Cliff said, turning to Collins.

"Well, as you might be aware," began Collins, "my home state of Arkansas has lots of wonderful and unspoiled waterfowl habitats. I want to do what is best to preserve these wild places for future generations to enjoy."

"I agree with that. What measures does it take to accomplish that end?" asked Cliff. He scanned their faces and could tell that Ellsworth the Sixth really had no idea.

"What it does is prevent existing habitat from being destroyed or misused, and takes measures to reward landowners for returning farmland to its natural state. This is conservation in action, Teddy Roosevelt style," said

Collins.

"So is the government going to add more land to the national parks system or something?"

"No, no, no," interjected De Luca. "The land stays in private hands, but these new regulations will assist landowners in determining the most environmentally sound ways to manage their property while still yielding a fair financial return."

"Who determines what fair is? That sounds a like roundabout way of saying that it puts new burdens on small family farmers who are trying to hang on."

De Luca smirked, "No Cliff, it's more of a partnership with the farmers. There is even a clause in the bill that gives landowners a tax break if they meet the standards."

Cliff could only guess how much Sherman had paid these two to write that in the bill.

"Not only will this legislation provide new tax breaks, it will also give free government-sponsored ecological consulting through our agricultural universities. Mississippi State, for example," said Collins.

Cliff nodded. He was saying that farmers would be suspect to regular inspections by some government bureaucrats who would slap them with fines if they didn't comply with his new bill. "Well that does sound like a good deal for everybody," Cliff lied convincingly. "But will it cost people their livelihoods? Spending money on improvements they can't afford in order to meet the new standards?"

"Oh no, we don't think so," said De Luca. "Quite the opposite. If they comply, it will prevent illogical use of the land. Nowadays we can squeeze out more yield per acre than ever before, making the land more valuable and therefore appropriating more money to the landowner and the farmer."

Cliff wasn't convinced. He knew there would be people who couldn't make the financial hurdle to comply. Then they'd either go into debt and risk foreclosure, or be forced to sell out. And guess who would be eagerly waiting to gobble it all up? Walton Sherman.

"Well it's about time we had some sensible leaders in Washington. Would you excuse me?" Cliff said and walked back inside the hotel. He went into the bathroom, making sure that he was alone. "Zoey do you hear me?" he said.

"Loud and clear," came her reply through the radio transmitter that was hidden inside his ear.

"Alright, bring in the package."

"On my way."

Back in the truck, Zoey picked up a small cardboard box and a clipboard with some official looking documentation on it, got out of the truck, and walked towards the hotel. Inside the cardboard box was another box, a ring box, and a forged note in a woman's handwriting. It read:

> Thomas I'm so proud of you. I got these for you to wear at the gala to remind you of all the beautiful wildlife you're protecting. I cannot wait to see you again.
>
> Your Beloved Angeline

Angeline was not the senator's wife. His marriage had been on the rocks for years. The only reason he hadn't gotten a divorce is because it would be political suicide in Bible-thumping Arkansas. Mr. and Mrs. Collins had kept their marital problems hidden fairly well, but not much could escape Marvin Cervantes and the FBI's vast hordes of digitalized information. Thomas Collins had kept several mistresses over the years, which was one reason his marriage had fallen apart in the first place. That, and the fact that his wife's libido had been nonexistent for the past two decades. Senator Collins had his girls on the side to gratify his desires.

Marvin had thought up this party trick. Inside the ring box were two silver cuff links shaped like flying mallard ducks that he knew Senator Collins would be happy to receive from his mistress. They were implanted with a microphone so Cliff and Zoey could record his conversations and hear everything that he said.

Zoey walked inside the hotel and up to the front desk. She laid the box on the counter. "I have a delivery for Senator Thomas Collins. It says that he's supposed to be at this hotel," she said to the desk manager while looking at her clipboard. "It's marked urgent delivery."

"Yes ma'am, we can certainly give that to him for you. Of course it will have to be checked by secret service before it can be delivered to the senator," the desk manager replied.

"Of course. I need someone to sign this saying that the package was received," Zoey said, and laid the clipboard on the countertop. She watched the desk manager sign the bottom of the page. "Thank you." Zoey took the clipboard and walked outside back to the truck.

Cliff was carrying on a conversation with a lobbyist on the terrace. He worked for some kind of group that advocated stricter environmental policy laws. He was pleasant guy from North Carolina and Cliff enjoyed talking with him because he had yet to bring up a political or litigious topic.

"I met my wife on jury duty," he told Cliff. "The reverend brought us together."

"That's unusual. Do tell," Cliff replied.

"Back where I'm from there was a preacher that had moved down from Detroit, specialized in marital counseling. You can only imagine why he wanted to get away from the city," the lobbyist grinned. "After a while, folks around town came to know him as Reverend Half and Half. He said above the waist he was all reverend, but below the waist he was man."

Cliff chuckled. "Uh oh."

"He was counseling one young couple and took a liking to this gal. She told him that she'd elope to California with him but she wouldn't be seen with a man who drove around in an old church van. So Reverend Half and Half devised a plan. He took a box of Little Debbies, wrapped it in duct tape, stuck wires all over it, and drove down to a bank. He put on a black toboggan and some big sunglasses, walked inside and laid his Little Debbie box on the counter, and told the teller that it was a bomb. He said that he'd blow the place sky high if she didn't give him some money. And not the fake kind!" the lobbyist laughed.

Cliff was listening while watching the senator talking with a group of people across the floor out of the corner of his eye. A young lady who was an employee of the hotel walked up said something to him, and Collins followed her out of the party.

"She filled a paper bag and he walked out with about forty thousand dollars," the lobbyist said like he couldn't believe it. "They caught him the next day at the Cadillac dealership trying to trade in the church van. Not only was his name not on the title, the license plate on the back said "Pryn4U".

He and Cliff both burst into laughter. "No it didn't," Cliff protested.

"Oh yes it did. At the end of the trial the judge asked him if he had anything to say before they took him to jail and he goes, 'For those who will hear, I'd like to recite from Paul's first letter to the Corinthians. Art thou bound unto a wife? Seek not to be loosed. Art thou loosed from a wife? Then seek not a wife!'"

He and Cliff both roared. The lobbyist said, "We both laughed so much during that trial that I asked her out after the sentencing and we've been together ever since."

"That's hilarious." Cliff chuckled. "Ole Preacher Half and Half."

"Reverend Half and Half," corrected the lobbyist.

Collins walked back in wearing the new cuff links, red-faced from alcohol, and smiling from ear to ear. He resumed his spot among the same people and showed off the new addition to his outfit. Cliff could hear their conversation. "Those are just darling!" said one woman. "A subtle display of personal flair," said another who sounded like she had spent most of her life in Newport, Rhode Island.

"Hey, it was great talking to you," said Cliff to the lobbyist. They shook hands and he dismissed himself. After Collins and his circle got off the subject of the cuff links, they resumed their normal pattern of conversation, name-dropping and gossiping about their political rivals. Cliff could hear Zoey snickering when one man bragged about "Gigging the shit out of some frogs with James Carville." Another said that she had once seen Margaret Thatcher naked.

Cliff looked around for Walton Sherman and couldn't find him. He became more conscious of the urge to relieve himself and went to the bathroom where he had summoned Zoey over the radio. He opened the door and discovered Walton Sherman standing at one of the St. Regis's ivory urinals. Cliff claimed the urinal beside him and said, "Hey bud," as he unzipped his fly.

Sherman looked over across the partition, startled and not pleased to be disturbed during such a moment. "Hey Cliff," he said dismissively.

"Listen, I've been thinking about that land you want to buy from me and I know that you have some personal reasons for wanting that property. I was hoping that we could meet up back in Memphis and talk about it. Maybe work out a deal that's good for both of us."

"Uh... sure," replied Sherman, a little embarrassed and looking at the ceiling.

"When can we do it?" asked Cliff ardently.

"I don't know, Cliff," said Sherman, anxiously straightening his pants and ready to get out of the bathroom.

"No seriously. We should have a meeting as soon as we can," said Cliff. Sherman didn't say anything and hurried to the sink. Cliff zipped his fly up and followed him. "Tuesday afternoon work for you? It does for me."

"Sure, sure Cliff that's fine," Sherman said, aggravated.

"Great! You know, I thought that you would be a little more excited about this." Cliff said as he dispensed soap onto his palm.

"I am, I mean I would've been had you asked me about it outside."

"Hey buddy, it's a natural thing. We all gotta go," Cliff reassured him. "So are you fired up about it?"

"Yes Cliff," Sherman said flatly.

"Good! Looking forward to it." Cliff turned the faucet off, shook his hands a few times, and then wiped them on a hand towel. Sherman started to walk to the door and Cliff called, "Hey, Mr. Sherman." He turned around. "Good talk," smiled Cliff. Sherman grunted and walked out of the bathroom. Mission accomplished. Cliff was done here. He walked out of the hotel and casually strolled the sidewalks of Washington, taking in the sights on his way back to the faux FedEx truck. Collins's voice and others buzzed unnoticed in his ear as Cliff listened in entertained silence. "Listen here, I've been around the Capitol for a while and I can tell you firsthand that even Dan Quayle could've beat your ass in Scrabble."

"I'm walking up behind you, let me in," said Cliff quietly. Zoey opened the back of the truck and he climbed inside. She shut the door. "Are you believing these people?"

"I'm not sure if I even want to be hearing some of this right now," Zoey laughed.

They listened for another hour in the back of the truck. Finally, they heard Sherman's voice. "Tom, can I borrow you for a few minutes?"

"Sure thing. Please excuse me, nice to see you." Senator Collins's sleeves swished as he walked. When it stopped they heard Sherman's voice again.

"Alright round everybody up, we need to talk business. The Azalea Room in thirty minutes. Let's make sure everybody doesn't go down there all at once."

"Don't worry Walt; we've all done this kind of thing before. Everybody knows how the game is played."

There was more shuffling and whisking as the senator made his way around the party. Every few minutes he would pull someone aside. "Azalea Room in twenty-five." "Azalea Room in twenty." A few people tried to initiate a conversation with him but he gently cut them short.

"Truman."

"Tom!" greeted Congressman De Luca.

The senator grabbed De Luca by the shoulder and closed in on his ear. "That girl you brought is a sexy little ole thing. You're going to have to let me in on which escort service you're using."

"Shhhhh," De Luca hissed. "People aren't supposed to be able to tell. That's why I pay extra for them."

"I'm the only one who can tell. I know you too well, Truman," the senator said in a chummy, hushed tone. "Be downstairs in ten minutes. It's time to go over the finances."

After shuffling another round through the terrace, a solid five-minute block of Collins's swishing sleeves filled the speakers inside the back of the FBI truck as he made his way to the Azalea Room. They heard a door open and close and then the lock of a deadbolt. "Is everybody here?" Collins counted quietly to himself, "One, two, three, four… Yep that's all twelve of us." He raised his hands for attention. "OK gentlemen, gathered in this room are influential members of both parties. We need you to use your votes and powers of persuasion to push the bill through both houses. With your support, *The American Waterfowl Habitat and Mississippi River Alluvial Plain Preservation Act* will be a magnificent bipartisan success. My friend Walton Sherman from Union Cotton has come here tonight to make the decision to support this legislation a very easy one to make. I'd like for you all to give him your attention."

There was a muffled bump as the senator's watch touched the top of the table when he sat down. He rested his elbows on the table with his hands together. The cuff links worked well and, unbeknownst to Collins, they were in a perfect position to catch them all in the act of committing a felony.

"Thank you, Tom," began Sherman. "The corporation I represent is very interested in protecting the environment, what we consider our nation's greatest asset. We hold that protecting America's abundant natural resources and indigenous wildlife should always be a top priority. With your support, we can conserve these resources and wild places for future Americans to use and enjoy. This bill needs to pass, and we support all of you using your influence to get it done. To ensure success, you will all receive half a million dollars, wired into the bank account of your choosing. Is that fair, gentlemen?"

There was a mumbled consensus and Collins spoke up. "Then it's settled. I'm happy to announce the passage of *"The American Waterfowl Habitat and Mississippi River Alluvial Plain Preservation Act."* Thank you everyone and enjoy the rest of your evening."

They all got up, and Zoey and Cliff listened to them adjourn. "Thanks for your support Marty, we should work together more," said Collins.

"I think so too. We'll be in touch."

"Who was that?" Zoey asked.

"Marty O'Donnell," Cliff replied, "a congressman from Oregon. Looks like a pasty Cee Lo Green."

"Good work, Truman," Collins said.

"Easy money," De Luca replied.

Other politicians were leaving but they didn't hear any sleeve swishing to indicate that Senator Collins was going anywhere. The door closed. "Alright Walt, we're getting it done," said Collins cheerfully. "You're going to make a Mama Cass buttload of money on this thing."

"Tom you are a true Boss Crump," Sherman complimented zealously. "We'll have a corner on the cotton market in North America. Nobody else will even come close. All those subsidies written into the thing will make it so we can't fucking lose! White gold my friend, and now we pretty much have a monopoly on it."

"Well it's always a pleasure doing business with you, sir. I might just have to go buy me a beach house in the Caymans so I can watch over all my funds!" Collins laughed.

"We've been doing business this way in my family for a long time. It pays to be the one pulling the strings," said Sherman.

"Old General Willy T. would be proud, wouldn't he?"

"He sure would."

Cliff and Zoey looked at each other. "What did that mean?" asked Cliff.

"I have no idea," she replied.

"I bet Marvin could figure it out."

"Probably. I'll get him on it. We should start heading back to Memphis. It's going to be a long haul." She looked into the rearview mirror at Chuck, the driver, who was bored and watching pedestrians in the rearview mirror. "Hey Chuck, take us home." He gave her a thumbs up and started the truck.

Zoey turned to Cliff. "It's a fourteen hour drive. Why don't you stretch out and get some sleep?"

"I think I will," said Cliff, plucking the radio transmitter out of his ear.

10

"Hey Marv," called Zoey as she and Cliff walked into his cubicle the next day.

He spun around in his chair. "Hey Zoey! Good job. That's exactly what we were looking for. This is going to be better than ABSCAM. Cliff, you were slick buddy."

"Thanks, Hoss Cat."

"Have you figured out what they meant by 'General Willy T. would be proud'?" asked Zoey curiously.

"Oh yeah," Marvin said, wide-eyed and wired on energy drinks. "Check this out." He spun back around and pulled up a black and white picture on his computer screen. "This is Civil War general William Tecumseh Sherman. Walt has a colorful family history, to say the least."

The bearded balding man in the picture sat in a uniform, straight and stiff with his arms crossed. He didn't look happy. "That's the guy who burned down Atlanta," said Cliff. "We had to learn about him in school because he occupied Corinth, where I grew up, after the Battle of Shiloh."

"Alright, so get this," said Marvin. "This guy is Walton Sherman's great-great grandfather. Union Cotton was officially organized as a legal entity by his grandson, Henry Leviticus McGregor, the illegitimate son of the general's youngest son, Philemon Tecumseh Sherman. Philemon inherited his father's estate despite being the youngest.

The general's eldest son, William Jr., died at the age of nine and then his next son Thomas received the birthright. Now, the General had high hopes for Thomas, probably aspiring for him to follow in his footsteps or go into law, but it didn't happen. Thomas chose a radically different path when he became a Jesuit priest, and that caused a great rift between him and his dad. The general's hopes of leaving a strong family line by Thomas were dashed because of the vow of celibacy that Thomas had to take to become a priest. So, most likely the general renounced any claims that Thomas had to the family inheritance.

The next son Charles died an infant, and finally Philemon was born. The general lived just long enough to see Philemon set up a successful law practice in New York City when he was twenty-four. So Philemon got the lion's share of the family's wealth, but he never got married and never had any children, save one."

"Henry McGregor," said Cliff.

"He didn't know who his father was until Philemon died in 1941 and left his entire estate to him. After he found out the truth, he changed his legal name to Sherman. Henry started Union Cotton in Memphis during World War II and they supplied cotton for army uniforms, bandages, you name it. Henry is Walton Sherman's grandfather. The interesting thing is, when Philemon died he owned tens of thousands of acres in Mississippi and West Tennessee that he passed down to Henry. But the man lived his whole life up north, mostly in New York."

"So Henry started Union Cotton from all that land," concluded Zoey.

"He did, and he beat other people's prices by being his own middle man. He made a lot of money selling the timber off of it too. Then he turned around and used that money to buy up more land."

"So how did a man who lived his whole life in the North come to own so much land in the South?" asked Cliff.

"I think he inherited it from the General. Before the Civil War, Sherman was the first superintendent of The Louisiana State Seminary of Learning and Military Academy, later to become LSU. While he was there he was known to be friendly to the southern aristocracy and had time to inspect the quality land in the South—perhaps he even developed a desire to own some himself. It's my guess that after the war he bought up a bunch of land cheap during Reconstruction."

"Huh," went Zoey, thinking it over. "Did he move back after the war?"

"No." Marvin shook his head.

"Then what was the point?" she asked.

"It was a store of value. There wasn't really much of a stock market to invest in at that time. He probably sharecropped it out or just let it sit. In people's way of thinking back then, owning land was the basis of wealth," said Cliff. "Union Cotton doesn't advertise that legacy," he pondered.

"Shoot," retorted Marvin. "Would you? No reason to explain yourself if you don't have to. Besides, the term 'carpetbagger' wasn't really something that drew positive connotations. Especially in the forties."

"Old Willy T. would be proud?" Zoey mumbled to herself.

"Marvin's right," said Cliff. "The general might have acquired that land through less-than-honest means. That's probably what they were talking about. Sweetheart deals were just a part of business back then. I wouldn't want to bring up a reason to smear my business's reputation either."

"We got 'em for bribery already. This is evidence of *quid pro quo*," said Marvin. "We could indict Sherman right now and he'd go to prison."

Zoey lightly touched her chin as she looked down, considering her options. "We can get more. Let's hold off on an indictment. I know we can get more."

"Someone wants to be director one day," Marvin quipped with a wink to Cliff. "Alright well what do you want to do?"

"Cliff, you approached him about having a meeting, right?" Zoey asked.

"Yes," Cliff snorted humorously. "I think we're having it Tuesday afternoon."

"You think you are?" asked Zoey.

"I'll call Leigh and get her to confirm it."

"Alright. Don't hesitate to lay the sweet talk on her," said Zoey.

•••

Monday at the office everyone was freaking because they'd seen his house on the news. Cliff had blasted out an email telling everybody that he was OK and that he was going out of town for the weekend to "clear his head." When he showed up in the morning, he was almost tackled by Sherri, the big hearted office manager who always wore enough bracelets to make Cliff think that a wind chime was coming down the hall. He had started moving some things upstairs little by little and decided to keep much of the big office much the same as Mr. Kenny had it, except he confined the stuffed iguana to the storage closet. He stole a few minutes of privacy from the hectic day to call Leigh.

"Hello?" she answered.

"Leigh, it's Cliff. How are you doing?"

"Cliff! I was hoping you would call me!" she said excitedly. "Just another lovely day. I've been talking to a four-and-a-half-foot-tall pig farmer from Paragould, Arkansas all morning. Told me to call him Big Un' 'cause everybody does," she laughed. "What's up?"

"Saw your boss this weekend. I told him I'd like to come in and talk to y'all about the offer you made me. We talked about doing it tomorrow afternoon. Can you confirm the meeting for me?"

"You went above my head, you ass?"

"I didn't mean to. I just ran into him and talked to him about it for a minute."

"'Oh. Yeah I guess I can do that for you. This deal seems to be a pet project of his anyway. I want you to serenade me again. You've got the passion of Meat Loaf, only you're really sexy."

"I don't know. You know I'd do anything for love… but I won't do that."

Leigh burst with laughter. "Oh yes you will."

"If you say so, Tina Turner. You really can sing your butt off. You even dance like she does."

"I dance better than she does. When will I see you again?"

"Tomorrow afternoon, I guess. You're coming to the meeting, aren't you?"

"Yeah I'll be there."

"By the way, I'm missing one of my favorite t-shirts. You wouldn't happen to know where it is would you?"

"The Ray Wylie Hubbard shirt?"

"That's the one."

"I have no idea," she kidded. In truth, she had stuck the shirt in her purse after spending the night with Cliff.

"Well I hate that. If you find it you can keep it. I'll see your fine ass in the board room."

"Alright," Leigh snickered. "Bye."

Was he really flirting with her? No, he told himself, no. She was one of the bad guys. Don't do that. It's OK, it's part of the sting operation. Zoey said to make her trust you. But I can't do that and fake it! Oh man, Cliff lamented, he was confused.

•••

The next day Cliff drove Mr. Kenny's Mustang east down Poplar Avenue into Germantown, an affluent suburb of Memphis. He turned onto a side road and then into the parking lot of an anonymous-looking office building. It was a six-story glass rectangle that had a parking lot filled with mid-range BMWs and Lexus SUVs. The outside of the building had no markings except for three numbers that told its address above the front door. There was nothing to indicate to the outside world that this building housed Union Cotton. Cliff parked and walked inside.

If the outside was unassuming, the inside was anything but. The lobby was a pristine, wood-and-mirror lined space with intricate crown molding. There were crystal chandeliers hanging from the ceiling. The dark stained reception desk had wooden resemblances of cotton plants raised slightly from its face in low relief. Cliff walked up and spoke to the receptionist. "Hello, I'm Cliff Carver. I have a meeting with Walton Sherman and Leigh Dalton this afternoon."

"Alright, let me see…" The young receptionist scrolled through her computer "Yes sir, they are expecting you. Go up to the top floor and the door will be right in front of the elevators."

"Thank you."

Cliff got onto the elevator, rehearsing how it would go in his mind. He was cool, confident, courageous, and cultured, he reminded himself. He checked the tiny microphone hidden underneath the lapel of his jacket. He took a deep breath as the elevator neared the sixth floor. The doors opened and he strode across the hallway and pushed open the left side of the double door in front of him.

Leigh, Sherman, and Arnold Hackworth waited at the other end of a long conference table. The far wall was composed entirely of glass, looking out onto the tall pines that shielded their business from the eyes of the public. Sherman held the gold coin in his right hand, caressing it with his fingertips.

"Hi Cliff!" Leigh was the first one to speak. She started to walk towards him in a professional-looking blue dress. She looked him in the eye on her way over, allowing a glint of passion from her irises that only Cliff could pick up on. She shook his hand and flashed a quick flirtatious smile, then assumed a straight-laced, all-business demeanor as she made introductions to the rest of the group. "I believe you know Walton Sherman, and this is our CFO Arnold Hackworth."

"Hey Mr. Sherman, good to see you again," grinned Cliff as he shook his hand. "Mr. Hackworth, glad to meet you."

"Let's all have a seat," said Leigh. "Cliff, can I get you some coffee or some water?"

"No. I'm fine, thank you," Cliff replied as he sat down next to Hackworth.

"Cliff, I'm glad we decided to do this," offered Sherman. He had his genial mask on now. He spoke clearly and energetically, like he was campaigning to be governor.

"Me too," said Cliff. "I've been doing some thinking about the offer that you made, Leigh, and I'm just curious to know a little bit more about what you'll do with the land once you have it."

Leigh and Hackworth glanced at Sherman. "Well that's a prime spot right there Cliff. We can farm it out and make money off of it and be over there to hunt in less than an hour. We've been enjoying that place for a long time and have grown quite attached to it. I'd really like to buy it. We made you an outstanding offer."

"Yes sir, it's a great offer, and I don't mean to press, so please excuse me if this is out of line, but why wouldn't you go buy another piece of land close by from somebody else? You could almost certainly get a better deal than what you've offered me."

Sherman smiled widely, concealing his true feelings behind a well groomed face. "Cliff, my father started leasing the hunting rights to that land a long time ago. I've hunted there my entire life and the best memories that I have of my father and me together all happened out there." He paused, thinking carefully about how to word his explanation, and his eyebrows drooped emphatically. "You see, my father was a hard man. He was never cruel to me or my sister or my mother, but he was always so stern, so serious, so unwilling to relax. At the duck camp he was a different person." Sherman held his hands up for emphasis and his eyes pleaded for Cliff's compassion.

"He was fun and energetic. He was the father that every young boy should be so lucky to have. I believe that when he went out there he felt, just for a little while, like he was the man he had once envisioned himself being before the weight of life had made him feel... trapped. To tell you the truth," he looked down for a moment, "and you might think that this is a little sad, all of the happy times I had with my father occurred somewhere on that property. Now that he's gone I like to remember him the way that he was when we were together at the hunting camp, not the way that he was in town. While that land may not be worth thirty million dollars on paper, it's worth every penny to me. Maybe now you can understand why I'd like to have it so much."

Man, that was a good speech, thought Cliff. Sherman sold the crap out of it. He might've even brought some people to tears on Oprah, but Cliff didn't believe that he was getting the whole truth. He decided to press a little more.

"Did you ever try to buy it from the Millwoods when they owned it?" he asked.

Hackworth's face tensed up a little for some reason, his mouth drew tighter, and his eyes were emotionless. Leigh and Sherman both had a look of sympathy on their faces after Cliff mentioned the name. "Yes I did," he said with concern. "I tried to buy it a couple times but they never wanted to sell it. I can't believe what happened," he shook his head sadly. "That's awful. Ronny Millwood had been a good friend to me. Always glad to see you and eager to help. He was a good fella," Sherman nodded with convincing sentimentality.

"Yeah," Cliff said kindly. "You know my boss Kenny McIntyre passed away recently. That land meant a lot to him, too. He was very excited about it but never got to use it. I think that it would be disrespectful to sell it so soon after all this has happened."

Sherman's gaze narrowed in soft disappointment. "I understand, Cliff. Let me tell you about my sister. She used to work here with me. Had a kind heart, always volunteering with charities and fundraising for St. Jude. She really loved other people. She died when our company plane crashed on the way back from a mission trip when she was forty and I was so conflicted on what to do with her house. She had bought this old Victorian that she spent years fixing up. She loved it, poured her heart into it. It kept me awake for weeks trying to decide what was the right thing to do with it." He clenched the coin in his fist like this was hurting him to talk about, trying to come across as a wise clergyman.

"Finally I decided to sell it and gave the money from the sale to St. Jude. Looking back now, I know that my sister would've been pleased with that and I know that I put way too much undue stress on myself about that decision. These things are hard, but time heals and we move on."

Did he have her killed too? That was the first thing that popped into

Cliff's mind. He wouldn't put it past him. Trying to tug on Cliff's heart strings wasn't working but he put on his compassionate look and nodded thoughtfully as if he bought it. "Well, let me offer a proposal that I think will satisfy both of us."

"Ok, let's hear it," said Sherman.

"Why don't we have a joint hunting club? You can buy fifty percent of the ownership from me and that way both of our companies can use it to entertain clients. We'd all meet some new people and I feel like we'd really get along. I think we'd have a lot of fun out there together. What do you say?"

Sherman smiled and turned the coin over in his hand. He put his elbows on the table and sat up straighter. He looked at Cliff, and in a warm and commanding voice said, "Cliff that is a tantalizing offer but I'm afraid we'll have to pass."

"We'll double your money," interjected Hackworth eagerly.

Cliff did his best to look disappointed. "I was really looking forward to sharing some good times together. I'm sorry you feel that way but I'm not interested in selling it outright. Um, if you change your mind please let me know," said Cliff with a gracious hand gesture.

"I hate that we couldn't come to an agreement Cliff. I guess we're done here," said Sherman. "Leigh, would you please escort Mr. Carver as he leaves?"

"I'd be happy to," she replied.

They stood up, and Leigh followed Cliff out of the conference room and into the elevator. When the door closed she lost her professional pretense. "Okay, now tell me what that was about."

"What was what about?"

"That in there! Why didn't you take the thirty million?"

"Why do you think Walton Sherman didn't want to be in a hunting club with me? I'm a little offended," he joked.

"I don't know. That all sounded pretty good to me. I thought he was going to say yes. I think he's just a control freak. But I still don't understand you. You could've had the nicest place money could buy with what we offered. Paid to build your man cave hunting lodge and everything!"

"Exactly! Why aren't y'all doing that? You can't tell me that a man like Sherman is willing to pay that much money simply for nostalgia."

"I don't know," she fussed. "They won't tell me, they just said they wanted to have it. Sherman and Hackworth make all those decisions. I just do what they tell me to."

"Are you lying to me?" he asked calmly but sternly. He couldn't tell if she was or not but he certainly wasn't about to trust her.

"No I'm not lying to you!" she cried. "Cliff, I was afraid you were dead!" she sniveled and tear fell from her eye.

He hugged her and pulled her close, and she looked into his eyes. "Shhhh. It's okay." He kissed her on the forehead. "The door is about to open."

They let go of each other and Leigh held her composure until they were in the parking lot. She walked him to the Mustang and they stopped before he got in.

"Cliff," she looked searchingly into his eyes, "listen, I'm feeling something for you. I don't know exactly what it is yet, but it's something that I haven't felt for anybody in a long time. Please tell me that you're all right."

Cliff took both of her hands and held them between his. "I'm fine. I am. I wasn't hurt. I barely made it out, but I wasn't hurt."

"What's going on Cliff?" she pleaded. "Are you mixed up in something? I'm not stupid. First your boss and then this?"

"I don't know, you tell me. Walton Sherman has been in the picture ever since these things started happening."

"What?" she recoiled. "Mr. Sherman wouldn't hurt anybody."

"I hope not."

"He wouldn't. Come on," she disapproved.

"You're right. I got to go."

"I'm sorry we couldn't do any business, Mr. Carver," she teased.

"I told you I don't like to talk about business when I don't have to," he smiled.

"Well then we should get together soon and talk about other things."

"We should." He leaned down and planted a kiss on her supple lips. "Have a lovely rest of the day, Ms. Dalton," he said, and got into the Mustang.

•••

In the conference room, Sherman was fuming. "Shit!" he rocketed up from his chair and slammed his fist into the table. "That smart-ass knows something. He knows more than he should."

"What do you want to do?" asked Hackworth from the side of the table.

"We'll sic the dogs on him," he said angrily. "They've been waiting for my go-ahead." Sherman pulled a cheap prepaid cell phone out of his pocket. "Time to let 'em eat. This ends today." He dialed a number and put the phone to his ear. "Hey. Y'all do your job. He just left the building." He clobbered the end button with his thumb and marched into the bathroom adjacent to the conference room.

Sherman dropped the phone on the tile floor and stomped it furiously into a pile of broken plastic. He took some paper towels and knelt down and swept up the pieces and dropped them into the trash can. Then he crumpled up more paper towels and threw them on top to cover any sign of the broken phone.

11

As Cliff drove down Poplar back towards downtown, he didn't at first notice anything out of the ordinary. The traffic wasn't that bad and everything seemed normal. A black Range Rover pulled out of a Chick-Fil-A parking lot and took a position in the westbound lane right behind Cliff's truck. Cliff was disappointed that he didn't get all the information that he wanted out of Sherman and the others. He was also disappointed that Sherman didn't agree to be in the club with him because they could have bugged the lodge. He would call Zoey later that afternoon; she would want to hear what he had to say about the meeting even though she had been listening in on the wire the whole time. Cliff reached down and turned the radio on, and Travis Tritt's soulful voice came floating through the speakers. "Call someone who'll listen, and might give a damn," sang Travis. Cliff began to sing along, "Maybe one of your sordid affairs, but don't you come around here handing me none of your lines, here's a quarter, call someone who cares."

Just as the chorus ended there were a few muffled pops and the Mustang's back glass shattered and something whizzed by his head. Ting! Ting! Ting! Ting! Cliff's hands locked onto the wheel and felt a sharp, intense spasm of panic. Ting! Ting! Ting! Ting! Ting! An acute blast of wind skidded by his ear. Gunshots.

He looked around wildly to see where the shots had come from. In his rearview mirror he glanced a man hanging out of the passenger-side window of the Range Rover behind him, wielding a sub-machine gun. Cliff looked ahead; he had a little room to run. He stomped on the gas, changed lanes and the Mustang's V-8 roared to life as he accelerated down Poplar Avenue.

The driver of the Range Rover was skillful and followed every move that Cliff made. Cliff tried to weave in and out of traffic, but it wasn't any use. The menacing black SUV stayed right on his tail, indifferent to other cars and the lives of the passengers in them. The gunner fired another burst, tearing off Cliff's passenger-side rearview mirror.

An intersection was coming up fast and the light was turning red. Cliff made it under the light just as it changed. The Range Rover scraped the front of an unlucky silver Toyota Camry that had impatiently blasted from the turning lane. The assassins didn't slow as they continued to pursue Cliff. They sprayed another volley of fire as the two vehicles shot past Overton Park.

Up ahead the light was red but Cliff took a hard left onto Mclean Blvd. The SUV didn't miss a beat, staying hot on his track and skidding through the intersection. Traffic was moving east and west ahead on Union Avenue but the cars in Cliff's lane were stopped. He charged into the middle lane and passed them, then slammed on the brakes and slowed down just enough to make the turn onto Union. As he screeched through the intersection, the Mustang grinded up the side of a pickup. After making the turn, another burst of fire tore into the back of the Mustang. The two vehicles careened down Union Avenue, dodging other cars like weaving rabbits. They tore through the medical district, passing the hospitals and then a park where a solemn stone statue of the Confederate cavalryman Nathan Bedford Forrest watched as the vehicles charged by in a blur.

Cliff's mind raced—he had to lose them somehow. Up ahead, a street took a forty-five degree angle off to the right and Cliff rumbled down it, passing Sun Studio, then erupted onto Madison Avenue and headed straight into the heart of downtown. He could see the high-rises up ahead getting closer as the muscle car roared towards them.

Adrenaline tweaking at his nerve endings, Cliff looked in his mirror and saw the Range Rover turn onto Madison Avenue, but he had separated the distance a little on them now. Desperately looking for an escape, he continued down Madison and the high-rises started to envelope him. The assassins were closing the gap and Cliff fiercely tried to speed up. The SUV was steadily pulling up beside him and its hood overtook Cliff's back bumper.

They fought for position, each vehicle banging into the other. The driver was now parallel with Cliff. He scanned desperately to his right and saw the man in the driver's seat; he noticed a tattoo on the inside of his right forearm as he gripped the steering wheel. It was a scorpion. No way. The auction! It was the stranger that Mr. Kenny had outbid! What the hell?

The stranger held the wheel with his right hand as he pulled out a pistol from the middle console and began to fire through the window with his left. The shots drilled through the passenger-side door, shattering the window, and a bullet ripped a gouge through the top of Cliff's right bicep. "Aaaaah-hhhh!" Cliff screamed in terror and slammed on the brakes. "Shit!" Cliff breathed fast and hard, blood pulsating from the hot wound as the Range Rover flew past him. They were in the heart of downtown and The First Tennessee Bank Tower loomed high above the Mustang. He turned left onto Third Street under the tower perilously and smashed into an old Chevy work van that was parked on the side of the curb.

The beat-up Ford kept plowing ahead, but it was a one way street and Cliff was going down it the wrong way. He almost collided with a car head-on but swerved to the left just in time to miss it—only to be greeted by a station wagon—then swerved back to the right and took a hard right turn down Monroe Avenue. The car barreled down Monroe and over 2nd Street, and Cliff waved his left hand fiercely, yelling "Move! Move!" at the pedestrians diving out of the way. He closed in on Main and had to slam the brakes to prevent himself from running into the back of the Main Street trolley as it passed in front of him. He got to Front Street and turned left, then dashed past the Cotton Exchange building where his office was, trying desperately not to hit anyone. If he could get on the interstate maybe he could last long enough for the state troopers to catch on and stop them.

The Range Rover appeared behind him again, bullets flying from both the driver and the passenger. Cliff gripped the wheel tighter. Blood from his arm was being slung all over the interior of the Mustang. He was losing strength in his right arm and it was difficult not to let it drop.

Cliff took a deep gulp of air; he would have to try something desperate here. He slammed on the brakes and at the same time turned the wheel hard to the right, afraid that he was about to flip. To his amazement, the Mustang slid around so it faced the opposite direction. He stomped on the gas and took off down the oncoming lane of traffic on Front Street. The Range Rover went past him but only for a second as the stranger mirrored Cliff's move and skidded the SUV around. "Damn!" Cliff yelled.

The passenger-side shooter shoved a new clip into the automatic weapon and unleashed another volley of fire, destroying the already-mangled trunk and taillights. The chase continued up Front Street, engines screaming. The Mississippi River was on their left, flowing south in the opposite direction. Cliff weaved to miss a sedan that was heading for him, taking a position in the north bound lane. Then he swerved back into oncoming traffic to overtake a slow-moving delivery truck. The assassins jerked around the truck, barely avoiding a head-on collision, and came up right behind Cliff once more. They passed the University Of Memphis School Of Law in the old federal court house, and Morgan Keegan Tower, a tapering, stair-stepped, brown office building, stood tall just ahead. Cliff took a hard right under its shadow heading east, back towards Main Street and the Lincoln-American building.

As he closed in on the intersection of Main Street, he could see the trolley that he had barely missed before lumbering down the rail line. He stomped on the gas and flew over Main Street, and the Range Rover chased him, narrowly missing the front of the trolley. Cliff took a hard right onto 2nd Street and darted around other cars, sprinting down the one-way over Madison Avenue and then Union Avenue, and then roared past the Peabody. He quickly slowed and turned into what looked like an alley as the Range Rover unleashed another torrent of bullets. The engine's rumble was made louder by the confined space between the buildings as Cliff darted towards the river. He crossed Main Street again and then Front Street as the bullets pounded his car and shattered the rearview mirror close to his face. When the pavement ended he frantically stood on the brakes, turned right, and skidded to a frenzied halt so he wouldn't stampede over the railroad tracks and into the river.

His chest pounded furiously and he was losing blood. Cliff hit the gas again, terrified, and heard the unsettling sound of crunching and twisting metal behind him. He looked and saw the Range Rover tumbling violently, tires over roof, down the riverbank. Cliff stopped the Mustang as the SUV made impact with the muddy water in a colossal splash. He gasped air rapidly and heavily as he watched the Range Rover sink into the river.

The high-pitched sounds of sirens overtook his consciousness as police cars careened in and surrounded him. The doors of the cars opened quickly, and police officers shielded themselves behind them with their pistols drawn and aimed at Cliff. "OUT OF THE VEHICLE NOW!" demanded a loud-speaker. Cliff felt like he was in a daze. He was weak. He stepped out of the Mustang and put his hands up. His vision was becoming blurry and his ears only buzzed. He felt dizzy. He looked around and saw "Gayoso Ave." on a green street sign before collapsing unconscious onto the asphalt.

•••

Late in the evening, Cliff sat upright on the hospital bed with his arm stitched up and bandaged tightly. Two police officers asked him questions. "Did you know the men in the vehicle that chased you?" asked one officer.

"No sir, but I had seen one of them before at an auction. I know it was him because of the tattoo on his arm."

"Did you provoke them in any way?"

"No!" protested Cliff. "It happened just as I told you."

"Alright, settle down," said the officer condescendingly. "How about the SUV? Had you ever seen that vehicle before?"

"No."

"OK. Mr. Carver why didn't you take more preventive measures to stop the chase sooner?"

"What?! What was I supposed to do? Wait still so they'd have a good shot?"

"Mr. Carver, don't take that tone with me. I'm afraid that we'll have to detain you, pending further investigation."

"But I didn't do anything wrong!" protested Cliff. "I was running for my life! You wouldn't have done anything different yourself."

"Reckless endangerment, property damage, speeding. The list goes on," patronized the other officer.

"I was trying not to DIE. You can't hold me in jail for running from people who were trying to MURDER ME."

"We'll let the courts decide that."

"That won't be necessary," said Chuck as he swaggered into the room. He had on a cheap black suit with a skinny tie and black sunglasses, and his beard almost touched his collar. He thought it was fun to play up his job, often acting like he was part of the *Men in Black*, which is why Zoey had relegated him to driver. "I'm Agent Charles Spreckels, FBI," he said in his most masculine voice. "Mr. Carver is with me." Chuck flamboyantly flashed around his badge.

The two startled officers looked at Chuck in shock, then at each other, then at Cliff. "Well I apologize Mr. Carver, we had no idea."

"It's alright guys, just doing your job. But you're making me angry for blowing my cover," Cliff responded in his toughest Dirty Harry.

"Well uh….. we're sorry. If you need any help or any information please don't hesitate to give us a call," said the second officer.

"From you two? Pssshhh," Cliff laid it on thick. "Don't waste my time. Let's go Chuck."

"See ya bitches!" yelped Chuck as they walked out.

Zoey waited in the backseat of her Tacoma in the parking lot. It was dark outside. Chuck went to the driver's seat and Cliff slid into the back with Zoey. Chuck started the truck and drove as Cliff and Zoey talked.

"Sorry I couldn't come get you myself. I've been working on this case too long to blow my cover," Zoey said. "So what the hell happened? It's been all over the news."

"I left the meeting with Sherman and everything seemed normal until I started getting shot at," Cliff quipped. "I didn't know what was going on. They stayed on my tail all the way down Poplar and through downtown, shooting the whole time. It's a wonder they didn't kill anybody." Cliff paused for a second. "And they totaled the Mustang! Fucking assholes!"

"Yeah, and they actually shot you in the arm, too," Zoey noted, as if Cliff had forgotten that part, and laughed.

"Yeah, that too. Sherman hired them. I know he did. The guy driving was the same guy that Mr. Kenny outbid at the auction. I didn't think about before, but he was probably at that auction representing Sherman."

"And Sherman didn't want to be there himself because...of...what?" Zoey asked slowly and contemplatively.

Cliff thought for a second. That was before Mr. Kenny, before he'd met Leigh, before he had been shot at, almost blown up, and scared out of his damn mind. He remembered that afternoon's meeting and suddenly it hit him. "Because he killed them." Cliff looked at Zoey in revelation.

"Who?"

"The Millwoods. The farmer and his son. I think he killed them, or had them killed. That's why he didn't want to be there himself. If anybody knew of his prior interest in that place it might have raised some unwanted questions. He said that he'd been trying to buy it from them and they wouldn't sell it."

"Whheeewww," Zoey blew a long, cognizant breath. "I think you might be on to something," she nodded thoughtfully. "That does make sense."

"Yeah. Sherman acted like they were all buddy-buddy at the meeting today. He's been hunting on their land his entire life so he knows that property like the back of his hand. If anybody could make those two particular people disappear without a trace, it would be Sherman," said Cliff with conviction.

"Do you have an idea of what he might've done with them?"

"No, not really," Cliff frowned. "But going by the recent experiences I've had, I don't think they're still alive."

"No," Zoey grazed her chin with her finger. "They're probably at the bottom of the river somewhere."

"Hackworth kind of tensed up when I brought up the subject too," Cliff remembered. "He knows."

"How are we ever going to get them to confess to that without any evidence?"

"I don't know." Cliff bit his upper lip gently. "They've got something going on out there that they don't want anybody else knowing about."

Cliff's phone buzzed in his pocket. It was Leigh. Cliff flashed the screen to Zoey and her eyes widened. "Answer it," she said eagerly.

He put it on speaker phone. "Hello?"

"Cliff! Are you hurt? It's Leigh," she sobbed.

"Leigh. I'm as good as I can be, I guess. What the hell is going on?" he demanded. "People have been trying to kill me ever since I met you."

"I don't know Cliff, I swear!" She was bawling. "I'm so sorry! I'm so sorry I got you into this!" She lost control and howled into the phone, "You've got to believe me!"

Cliff looked at Zoey and she mouthed, "Be nice." He nodded and gathered himself.

"I want to. Where are you?"

"I'm in my car. Cliff I'm so worried! They won't tell me anything! I don't know what to do! I don't know what's going on! I feel like this is all my fault!"

"Calm down," he said reassuringly. "Pull over somewhere. You don't need to be driving. Tell me whatever you do know."

"Let me come meet you somewhere. I don't feel safe."

Zoey was nodding so hard her body was bouncing up and down in the seat. "Your Office!" she mouthed. "Your Office!"

"Okay. Do you know where my office is?" asked Cliff.

"No," she sniffed.

"It's in the Cotton Exchange building on the corner of Union Avenue and Front Street in downtown. I'll be there to let you in. Try to relax, don't get in a wreck."

"I'll be there in a minute. Cliff I'm so sorry! I'm so sorry!" she whimpered.

"It's alright; everything is going to be alright. See you in a minute." He hung up the phone. "Chuck, you know how to get there?"

"Oh yeah, I'm a human GPS, dude," he replied, and turned around.

•••

Cliff was waiting in the ground floor lobby when Leigh knocked on the door. He was wearing the bug underneath the tail of his untucked shirt. Zoey was around the corner in the hall to the bathrooms and Chuck loitered on the streets outside, making sure that Leigh hadn't been followed. Cliff opened the door, and Leigh ran into him and embraced him. He held his arms in the air but didn't hug her back, he just couldn't bring himself to do it. She cried with her face buried in his chest. "Cliff! Thank God! I didn't want any of this to happen, I swear!"

"Let's go upstairs," he said.

She looked up at him and nodded. What little makeup that she had on was smeared and running down her face. "Oh God! What happened to your arm?"

"They shot me," said Cliff matter-of-factly. They stepped into the elevator and Cliff started frisking her. "Are you wearing a wire?"

"No! You don't trust me?" she blubbered.

"I don't have a reason to," he said flatly, and continued to check her. She was clean. The door opened to the tenth floor and they stepped out. Leigh was shaking nervously as they walked into Mr. Kenny's—now Cliff's—office. "Sit down," Cliff directed. He sat across from her. "Tell me what you know."

"I'm telling the truth Cliff," she sniveled. "I'm scared. They wouldn't talk to me all day today after you left. Everybody saw the chase on the news and..." her voice trailed off. "I thought about what you said, and I know that Mr. Sherman had to have something to do with it. You were right!" She started to cry loudly again. "I don't know how this happened. It seemed like such a good job," she lamented between broken sobs with her head down. "Cliff, believe me! Please," she pleaded. "I was just doing what I thought was my job. I had no idea it would lead to all this."

"Yeah, okay," said Cliff unsympathetically.

"What do I have to do to make you trust me!?" she screamed, and looked up at him with red eyes.

"Tell me something I can use against Walton Sherman."

"Like what?"

"You got any dirt on him? Know any of his secrets?"

She shook her head and sniffed as the tears slowed. "No, he's a very private man." She rubbed her eyes.

"Who would know something?" Cliff asked.

"That would tell? Oh I don't know." She looked to the side in thought. "I can't think of anyone."

"Does he have any enemies?" Cliff crossed his arms.

"I… I'm not sure. Not that I'm aware of."

"Think hard. Take your time."

Her eyes narrowed in concentration and then opened back up like a light bulb went off above her head. She looked back at Cliff. "There is one guy that would probably want to see him go down."

"Who?"

"Clyde Peterman. He got sent to jail in Mississippi and I was hired to replace him."

"What he do?"

"Killed a prostitute in a motel room. They say he chopped her to pieces. Something awful."

"My God," Cliff uttered, disgusted. "Do you know anything else about it?"

"I know he pleaded innocent. People at work say he was nice guy. He had a pretty wife and two young boys. Now he's on death row in Mississippi." Leigh sat up in her chair and readjusted herself.

"Did you go to the trial?"

"No, but some of the people who did said he denied it over and over again. He had an outburst or two in the courtroom. Mr. Sherman was a witness, and I heard that Clyde Peterman called him a son-of- a-bitch while he was on the stand."

"Uh-huh," said Cliff, thinking. "And he's on death row?"

"Yeah."

"Sounds like somebody who would be willing to unload some dirt on Sherman. I'm going to go see him."

"You're going to the jail?"

"Yeah. I want to talk to this guy."

"Where is it? Where are you going?" she asked.

"To the Delta. Death row in Mississippi is at the Mississippi State Penitentiary, Parchman Farm."

12

Cliff rolled along the flat, straight road in a silver unmarked government Ford Expedition heading south from Marks, Mississippi. He was deep in the Delta, right in the heart of Sunflower County. It was a Tuesday. Inmate visits were only allowed on the first and third Tuesdays of the month. This part of Mississippi is about as rural as rural gets. Escapees could run for days out in the open—without much protection from trees in the sweltering sun—die of a heat stroke, and not have gotten anywhere in particular. Cliff could see why the state felt no need to put a fence around the property of Parchman Farm. It used to be hard to hide from a bloodhound, but now it was nearly impossible to hide from a helicopter. If a prisoner did get out, there wasn't anywhere for him to go.

The square fields like a giant irregular checkerboard passed by the windows until finally he saw a green and white road sign that read "PENITENTIARY AREA - EMERGENCY STOPPING ONLY - NEXT 2 MILES". There was an old concrete gate up ahead on the right side of the road with a small guardhouse underneath it. Beyond the gate was a straight road that led into the heart of the penal farm. For about a hundred yards the road was lined with tall oak trees and tiny brown houses on either side. The sign above the gate read "Mississippi State Penitentiary".

Cliff turned the truck right, pulled up to the gate, and rolled his window down. The guard was an overweight woman who asked him, "What you here for?"

"I'm here to visit somebody," Cliff answered.

She snorted. "Need to see some ID." Cliff shifted in his seat, pulled his wallet out of the back pocket of his slacks, and handed the woman his driver's license. The guard inspected it and then wrote something on the top slip of a stack of large yellow notecards. She handed Cliff back his license and the yellow card, which was a pass to get inside the prison.

"Stick that up on your dashboard, can't have a vehicle in here without one. Make sure you put it where they can see it."

"Will do it. Thanks," said Cliff.

He placed the yellow card on his dash, the guard opened the gate, and Cliff drove through. The small cracker-style frame houses on the right and left side of the road were bordered by seemingly endless fields of bare, disked-up earth beyond to the north, south, and west. Cliff guessed that state employees lived in these houses. Parchman was far enough away from anything that it justified building a little community for the people who worked at the prison. He didn't see a school—maybe the kids were bussed to Drew or Ruleville, he wasn't sure. On the left side of the road was a low-slung, brown brick administration building with several metal garages behind it. They were all enclosed within a tall chain-link fence topped with razor wire. Several new and older model pickups were parked inside the fence behind the building. Cliff pulled into a parking space labeled "VISITOR" beside two Mississippi State Trooper patrol cars in the front lot. There were no other vehicles besides the cruisers, so Cliff figured he must be the only visitor there.

He got out and felt the late summer humidity set heavy on his skin. He grabbed the handle of the glass front door, pulled it open, and walked through. Inside, there was a waiting room with old, sturdy wooden chairs and one ancient, rusting water fountain. The opposite wall had a bulletproof glass partition with a hole about the size of a grapefruit cut in the center of it. Behind was a countertop that served as a desk, at which sat a slightly overweight older man. He had on a khaki shirt with a patch sewn on the upper right chest in the shape of the state of Mississippi that read "Mississippi State Penitentiary."

"What can I do you for?" asked the man from behind the glass, looking oddly at Cliff as he walked up. Cliff noticed that something wasn't exactly right about the man's face. His right eye was opened wide and the skin around his left eye sagged unnaturally.

"I want to speak to Clyde Peterman," Cliff answered.

"Clyde Peterman?" asked the man, surprised. "What business do you have talking to somebody on death row?"

"I just want to ask him a few questions."

"You some kind of lawyer?"

"No. I just want to see if he knows somebody that I know."

"You must be running with the wrong crowd, then."

"I've been getting that feeling here lately."

The man eyed Cliff warily. As he did, Cliff noticed a faded scar that ran from his forehead above his left eyebrow, across the skin around his left eye socket and down his cheek for a little ways, stopping before it reached his nose. The man's left eye was stagnate and didn't move as the right one did. It was glass, Cliff realized. His real eye had probably been gouged out in a prison riot or something. Maybe he had gotten shanked. "Hang on just a minute," said the man.

The guard picked up a landline office phone and pressed a button on the old phone's boxy dashboard. "There's a fella here who wants to speak with Clyde Peterman," said the man into the phone with obvious disdain and looking at Cliff with a questioning eye. "Alright, see you in a minute." He hung up. "Jeb will be on out here in just a second. He'll drive you back there. You just sit down and wait on him now." He spat into a trash can beside him.

"Thanks," said Cliff, and sat down in one of the stiff wooden waiting chairs. The chairs had small carvings all over them. Expletive words, black power fists, swastikas, an image of stick man raping another stick man. After Cliff had sat there for a few minutes a young prison guard dressed in a black uniform came out of the door beside the desk. A bulletproof vest bulged from beneath his short sleeved button-up. He had a pistol in a black leather holster on his belt, handcuffs, and a boxy radio attached to the other side. "You the fella he called me about?"

"Yes sir," replied Cliff.

"Jeb Walker," he said without the slightest attempt at friendliness. "Stand up, I got to pat you down before we go any further, make sure you ain't got no firearms or nothing. Standard procedure."

Cliff stood up and held out his arms. The young guard proceeded to do a quick search. He pulled both legs of Cliff's pants up above his pink and green striped socks and pulled them back down. He ran his hands up Cliff's sides, under his arms, down his back, and on the insides of his thighs. "Alright, you good. Take everything you got in your pockets and hand it to the man back there."

Cliff took out his cell phone, car keys, pocketknife, and wallet. He handed the things through the hole in the glass two at a time. The one-eyed man took them and put them in a drawer under the counter. "You'll get 'em back when you come out," he said.

"Follow me," commanded Walker.

He led Cliff through the door beside the bulletproof glass and down a hallway to the fenced-in yard in the back. They got into a single-cab fleet truck with a steel lattice partition between Cliff and Walker. They drove out of the gate, past the tiny houses, and deeper into the vast property. Cliff expected to see a chain gang plowing up these fields with garden tools but didn't. The ACLU had put a stop to that, although this place was a working plantation for more than one hundred years.

"Why you wanna be talking to Clyde Peterman?" asked Walker from the other side of the lattice.

"I just want to ask him some questions. See if he knows anything about a mutual acquaintance."

"Uh-huh," grunted the guard, tongue-in-cheek. "So you know him?"

"No. Never met the guy, but I know people that he used to know."

"Well, I don't know much, but they say he used be in with some powerful folks."

"I wouldn't know anything about that. I just need to know what he knows about a guy who wants to do some business with us. Not sure if it's a good idea or not."

"If you got to talk to a guy in prison about somebody, it's probably not a good idea to be doing business with them."

"Point taken. What can you tell me about Clyde Peterman?"

"That guy is different than the other boys they got in here," said the guard.

"What do you mean?" asked Cliff.

"Just the way he carries himself. He isn't a skinhead. Usually if you're white in this place, you're some backwoods meth-cooking shit or Aryan Brotherhood white trash. He isn't. He's smart and very white collar, no tattoos or nothing. He isn't the kind of guy you'd expect to wind up in this place."

"What did he do? I don't really know all the details."

"Found him in a cheap motel in Byhalia with what was a left of a whore. When the police got there he was just coming 'round, had a ton of drugs and alcohol in his system. He said he didn't do anything and didn't even know who that woman was. He cried like a baby but it didn't convince anybody. They caught him red-handed. His fingerprints were everywhere. There was no way he was getting out of it."

"What was his story?" asked Cliff.

"Ask him yourself. We're almost there."

They turned right down a hard-packed dirt road that intersected the fields like a dusty vein. There were two walled compounds in the distance, one to the right and one to the left. They were spaced about 200 yards from each other, and a tall stone wall with concertina wire on the top ran all the way around each one of them. There were guard towers in each of the four corners of the two compounds. The truck turned at a ninety-degree angle and went towards the buildings on the right, Area 1.

Walker pulled the boxy radio from his belt. "Officer Walker requesting Entrance to Area 1."

A voice came back over the radio, "You in the white truck?"

"That's us."

"I see you. Permission granted," the voice squawked.

There was a parking lot full of vehicles across the road from the heavy solid iron gate. Walker pulled the truck into the lot and parked, and the two men walked across the road in the sweltering heat. They stepped up to the guardhouse where a stocky, mean-looking officer sat. A window-box air conditioner was blasting his face with a frigid, manufactured breeze. The guard's short sleeves halfway covered the tattoos on his upper arms, and he was spitting tobacco juice into an empty Gatorade bottle. "What y'all down here for?" he asked Walker.

"Got a guest for Clyde Peterman."

"Damn it. People just can't help themselves from stirring up shit," the guard glared at Cliff.

"Let's just get it fuckin' over with," said Walker.

"Alright, alright. You know the drill," said the guard, and spit into the plastic bottle. He pushed a button on his right and the first set of heavy gates swung open slowly. Cliff followed Walker through and they closed, then another gate opened in front of them to let them inside. Tall steel fencing topped with more concertina wire ran around the inside of the thick stone wall. Guards brandished high powered rifles from atop the towers. Prisoners did push-ups and lifted weights inside of a chain-link cage, and a group of skinheads were tattooing Teutonic crosses on their necks with salvaged parts from old ink pens. In front of them were concrete block bunkhouses interconnected by walkways, and in the center was a larger building that Walker and Cliff went inside.

Walker led him through a series of locked doors and then back outside and down a path enclosed with more steel fence, like a tunnel. When they reached the other end they were in front of a reinforced concrete building in the back of the compound. There were two guards standing on each side of the maximum security door that led into death row. Walker spoke to the guard on the right. "This is a visitor for Clyde Peterman. Requesting entry into Unit 29."

The guards gazed at Cliff like he was the lowest, most repulsive life form on Earth. "You got a card from the warden?"

"Yeah." Walker drew a white notecard out of his breast pocket and handed it to the man, who looked it over.

The guard held the card up in front of a security camera and called on his radio, "Requesting entrance into Unit 29."

"Permission granted," the radio cackled back.

They heard a turning of gears and shifting of bolts as the door unlocked. The guard took the heavy door by the handle and held it open as Walker and Cliff went through it, and then he closed them in. There was no sunlight inside of the door, just the stinging glare of many long fluorescent tubes. The concrete walls were painted flat white and the space was illuminated so brightly that it was eerie, like a giant operating room. Cliff blinked in an effort to get his eyes to adjust. There were rows of cells going down one side of a wide central room, top and bottom, with solid steel doors. There looked to be around fifteen cells in each row, estimated Cliff, so thirty to a side. There were no windows in the doors, just a small slot at the bottom of each one that only slid open from the outside so that the guards could kick cold food in. Directly across from Cliff was a metal door, but it was not the same as the doors on the cells and it had a small reinforced glass window in the top half. Two sets of metal stairs rose up on each side of it, leading to concrete walkways that went along the top row of cells with gleaming metal rails lining their edges.

"Howdy Jones, Rowdy, Two Bit," said Walker to the guards inside.

"Hey," said one of the guards, peeling his shoulder blades off the white wall and swaggering towards them. He was a big, tall man and obviously in charge. "What y'all here for?" he asked as he was halfway across the floor. His colleagues followed him over.

"Fella here wants to talk to Clyde," said Walker.

"Well that can be arranged, I reckon," he said as he came to a halt, looking at Cliff with hard, judgmental eyes. "Y'all take him back there to the room."

"This way." Walker ushered Cliff towards the windowed door in the center across from them. Beyond the door on the right was a room separated into two halves lengthwise by a thick reinforced glass wall. On either side of the transparent barrier was a stainless steel counter that ran the length of the glass. One chair was in the exact center of the counter on each side, bolted to the floor. Resting on the counter in front of the chair was a blocky phone anchored by a thick wire. "Sit down," directed Walker. Cliff sat and Walker and the tall guard stood behind him, far enough away so they weren't breathing down his neck, but close enough for Cliff to feel their looming presence.

He waited until one of the guards brought Peterman through a door on the other side. Peterman was wearing a bright orange jumpsuit and his wrists and ankles were chained. He was clean-shaven, average height—around five-foot-ten—wore plain looking glasses, and had graying black hair. He wasn't a scary-looking man; he looked, rather, like a boring suburban father of two. Something that did strike Cliff were his excruciatingly sad eyes. They looked as if an unbelievable weight was pressing down on him with no hope of ever having relief; he looked like a man wishing to die whom death will not come to fast enough. Peterman sat down in the chair across the glass and picked up the phone. "Who are you?" he asked, sounding pissed off. "I've never seen you before in my life."

"My name's Cliff. I'm a commodities trader in Memphis."

Peterman huffed. "A white collar brat just like I used to be. What brings you down to the sun and fun of Parchman Farm?" he asked with indignation. "You're the first person from outside this prison that I've talked to since I've been here."

"I know somebody you know, somebody that I think is up to something crooked."

Peterman laughed. "Shit, that doesn't surprise me. Who is it?"

"Walton Sherman."

Peterman's eyes suddenly changed. His pupils got smaller, more concentrated, and his eyelids narrowed. He clenched his jaw and scowled. "What do you want to know about that fucker?"

"I know for a fact that he has tried to have me killed. I also suspect that he's killed others. I think he's hiding something and I don't know what that is."

"Not the first life he's ended. That son of a bitch is the reason I'm in here. He is the reason my kids don't have a daddy anymore. Ask me anything and I'll try to answer it. Anything to bring that piece of shit down."

"What happened that night?" asked Cliff.

Peterman's scowl softened and his brow tightened as he recalled the painful memories. Cliff could tell he had told this story before, hundreds of times. He probably went over it in his mind every day. "I had just closed a big deal with Archer Daniels Midland. Sherman was especially perked up that day, slapping me on the back about eight or nine times throughout the afternoon. I could tell that something was going on, that he was faking a little bit, because he was overdoing it. It was a Friday and Walt insisted on taking me out that night. He said he wanted to celebrate in high style."

"What'd y'all do?"

"Have you seen his car?" Peterman raised his right eyebrow.

"No."

"The guy has an extended wheel base Rolls Royce Phantom that he gets out of the garage for special occasions. It's pure luxury. He doesn't drive it. He has a guy that he calls up whenever he wants to use it that drives him around."

Cliff nodded, encouraging Peterman to continue.

"His driver picked us up from the office at the end of the day. I thought he wanted me to ride with him so he could talk about giving me some kind of raise." Peterman's gaze drifted off to his right. "We got into that Rolls Royce and pulled out of the parking lot, and he kept talking about how pleased he was with the ADM deal and how I was such a great asset to the company and all this other bullshit. When we got on Poplar he pulled a bottle of thirty-year-old scotch and two whiskey glasses out of a console in the backseat. He said he wanted to toast my success." Peterman sneered insolently while bobbing his head, then he took a slow, deep breath.

"Right before he was going to hand the glass to me he pointed out the window on my side and went, 'Whoa, that's a badass ride. Look out your window, Clyde.' I looked and there was a silver Aston Martin driving in the lane beside us. It was cool enough to hold my attention for a few seconds. I'm positive now that he had somebody driving it just to distract me so he could slip something in my scotch. He had it all planned out. When I looked back he handed me the glass and smiled. Then he said something I'll never forget." Peterman looked down with a smirk and shook his head.

"He said, 'A toast to a bright future, and great career. We plan to have you with us for a long time, Clyde.' Then we touched glasses and we each took a sip. I remember riding in the car for a few more minutes and Sherman rattling on with his bullshit. I took one more sip of scotch and it all went blank. I don't remember anything at all from that time until I felt a cop bashing me on the head on a bloody motel room carpet."

"You don't remember anything?" Cliff pressed.

Peterman shook his head. "Not a damn thing. I know Sherman put something in that drink. I know he did. I know he killed that prostitute, too. I told the lawyers, I told the judges, I told everybody that I could, and nobody even lifted a finger to look into it. He had the whole thing rigged like a well-oiled machine. The trial went down smooth and quick, and it didn't take 'em long to throw me in this place. There wasn't an investigation. They just saw the fingerprints and me passed out in that motel room and it was over. It all happened just like Sherman wanted it to, the puppet master. He had all of 'em in his back pocket. Seems like justice can be interpreted by the highest bidder down here."

Cliff nodded gently. "I can believe it. I've seen enough of Sherman and the way he operates to know that what you just told me isn't unlikely. If you help me maybe I can get you out of here and we can put Sherman behind bars where he belongs. We'll try to get you back to your family so you can be a husband and a father again."

Peterman looked back at him with a glimmer of hope and happier than he'd probably been in years. "I'll tell you whatever I know."

"Why would Sherman have a reason to want you out of the way?"

"Because he knew I knew."

"About what?"

"I walked in into his office one day without knocking and I overheard him talking on the phone to somebody about getting rid of that old farmer over in Arkansas, Ronny. Some contract killer or something. He had his back turned to me and was looking out the window. He didn't even realize I was there for a minute or two. By the time he turned around he had said enough for me to get the hang of what he was talking about."

"How long ago was this?"

"It was around three years back now."

"So you knew Ronny?"

"Yeah I knew him. He's a great guy. Simple fella, but he was never worried about anything. Union Cotton leases his land to hunt on."

"He's dead, Clyde. His death, in a roundabout way, is what brought me into this mess."

Peterman broke eye contact for a few moments and his face reddened in anger as his jaw tensed up. "Well, with me locked up in here I guess there wasn't anybody to blow the whistle. I tried to tell my lawyer but he wouldn't listen."

"Killed his boy too. His wife decided to sell the farm after they disappeared and my boss outbid Sherman's man and bought the place. Then my boss wound up dead."

"Aw man, Aw man," Peterman shook his head hotly. "Sherman's responsible for it, I guarantee you. He has guys that do that kind of thing. Professionals."

"So Sherman had been thinking about getting rid of Ronny Millwood for a while?"

Peterman nodded. "I'm surprised it took him this long. I guess he wanted to let everybody forget about my trial. Having an employee accused of murder wasn't great press for them, I'm sure."

"Didn't you tell the jury your story?" inquired Cliff.

"Through some legalese they made sure I never had an opportunity to testify. The judge told me, 'since you say you don't remember anything, you must not have anything to say.' I tried to yell it out in the courtroom, but as soon as I did they shut me down. The guards drug me out of there before the jury had a chance to hear anything. My lawyer didn't object to any of it, he didn't try to help me a bit. Whatever I paid him I bet Sherman paid him three times as much to make sure I got convicted, and I paid him a lot of money. He was supposed to be a good one."

"Why do you think he wanted Ronny gone?" asked Cliff.

"He wanted his land, obviously. He's been trying to get it for years, but I guess you figured that out the hard way."

"Yeah. What's he doing out there? There has to be a reason he wants that particular piece of property so badly."

"He's hiding something. He doesn't talk to anybody about it; at least he sure as hell didn't want me to know about it."

"What do you think it is?"

"I'm not sure exactly. He would always act a little paranoid whenever Ronny came around at the hunting camp, though. My guess is that it has something to do with that coin he's fidgeting with all the time. Whenever Ronny showed up he would put it away, like he didn't want him to see it. But I've never been around him when he didn't have the coin on him. He always seemed to have it out when he was on Ronny's property, just never when Ronny was around. He's always flipping it, and playing with it, and rubbing it between his fingers. Kind of weird, you know? He usually seemed like he was nervous about something out there, like there was something about that place he knew that none of us did and he was scared of someone finding out."

"I've seen him with that coin," Cliff acknowledged. "Do you know what it is exactly? Why he keeps it on him?"

"See, you know what I'm talking about. It's a Liberty Head Double Eagle, family heirloom. They started minting them during the California Gold Rush. Some fathers pass down watches, it seems the Shermans pass down old coins. It stays with him all the time, like it's a good luck charm or something. You know, Walt's daddy was the one who started that club way back when. They picked that particular spot to hunt for a reason, I guarantee you. Whatever it is, it's been going on for a long time."

"Any idea of what that could be? Even if it's just a hunch, even if it seems unimportant, please tell me. Anything could be a clue."

Peterman looked a little embarrassed and reluctant.

"What?" Cliff grinned a little. "I'm not judging you. Tell me."

"Well, there is one thing," Peterman began. "It's a wild guess, but I have a lot of time to use my imagination in this place."

"Go ahead," Cliff prodded.

"Sherman has some kind of obsession with this old steamboat that sank in the Mississippi River in 1865 called the SS *Sultana*. He has several models of it and all these old and obscure books… captains' logs… and navigation charts from the Civil War. It's all in his study at his house, the same study that his daddy used for years, I'm guessing. It's so much stuff you'd think he was writing a dissertation on it. He lives in the house he grew up in, a big ole place in Chickasaw Gardens near the Pink Palace."

"His wife had talked him into having a party for all the 'society people', you know," Peterman rolled his eyes. "I had just started working at Union Cotton and he invited me to go." He flipped his cuffed hands up. "I got bored and just wandered in there, into the study. It's a neat-looking room, wood paneled with floor to ceiling bookshelves. I couldn't help myself, I was so intrigued I had to check it out. All this stuff about the shipwreck was spread all over the table. There were open books with lithographs and maps from the eighteen hundreds that somebody had been marking all over with a red pencil. I started flipping through some of it, I mean I thought it was pretty cool, you know?" Peterman shook his open palms, hoping to garner some understanding from Cliff.

"Sherman came walking down the hall and saw me in there and freaked out. He tried to act cool, but I could tell he was pissed. He ushered me out of there real quick. I tried to ask him about it. I didn't know him real well back then and I thought that it was something that he might enjoy talking about. He just told me it was a hobby, and he never would talk about it again. I wouldn't be surprised if me seeing all that stuff might've added some fuel to his fire for throwing me in here."

"Huh," Cliff grunted, fascinated. "What does that have to with him killing Ronny Millwood?"

Peterman leaned forward. "Have you ever looked closely at his gold coin?"

Cliff shook his head, "Nope. Never really had the opportunity."

"The date on it is 1865. It's almost rubbed off, but it's there. The same year that the *Sultana* sank."

"You think there's some kind of connection?"

"Maybe. I mean, he really did have tons of research on that one event. I think he knows where it is, or maybe his daddy figured it out. The river is only a mile or two east of the camp house. I think he wants that spot to set up shop for some kind of excavation without people asking too many questions."

"For a Civil War riverboat full of gold?" Cliff asked, the disbelief coming through in his voice.

Peterman nodded. "Oh you might think it's stupid, but I think that's what the whole intention of that place was to begin with. The Shermans just figured the Millwood family would sell it to them eventually, but they wouldn't. I don't think I'd want anybody finding out about it if I discovered a shipwreck full of treasure. It'd be all over the news, you'd have rednecks trespassing trying to get a piece of it, the government would come claim it and confiscate it, there'd be a ton of legal shit to deal with. No," Peterman shook his head. "It's best to keep that under wraps."

"So that's why he wanted them dead, then?"

"That's what I think. Ronny was rooted, talkative, and he asked a lot of questions," Peterman concluded.

Cliff scratched his head.

"Wish I could do that," quipped Peterman, holding up his chains.

Cliff blew a puff of air from his nose and showed a small, sympathetic smile. What else could he ask him? Try to get as much from him as you can, he told himself. Cliff thought for a brief moment. "Does the word Gayoso mean anything to you?"

Peterman nodded, "Yeah. That's the name of the old hotel Sherman bought."

"Old hotel?" Cliff said, surprised.

"Well it's not anymore. He renovated it and turned it into apartments. It's in downtown Memphis, pretty close to Beale Street. I'll tell you though, I think he just bought it so he could have the basement." Peterman's lips curled perceptively and his eyebrows perked up.

"Why?"

"He's into bullion trading. Gold, silver, precious stones. When I was working for him he was always flying to New York to meet with a group up there that he was in with." He paused, trying to remember. "Avalon Bullion? Avalon Gold? Avalon something or other," he squinted with his head down, and then looked back up at Cliff. "Anyway, he's a collector. I always thought he bought that building so he could put a vault in the basement while he was renovating it without anybody knowing about it. I didn't think about it till they locked me up in here, but he probably wanted a place to keep gold from the *Sultana*."

"Come on..." said Cliff skeptically.

"I'm telling you, man," Peterman nodded. "It sounds far-fetched, but that guy has some expensive hobbies. That's the only time I've ever heard the word Gayoso."

Cliff nodded, trying to decide whether he believed him or whether he thought that the bright, sterile lights in here had zapped Peterman's brain. "Anything else I should know?"

"No. That's all I got man, I hope it helps."

"Thanks Clyde, it does. Keep your hopes up. Maybe I'll get to see you again outside these walls."

"I hope so. Are we done?"

"Yeah, I guess so."

"Alright." Peterman stood up and the guard escorted him through the back door. Walker led Cliff back the way they had come and finally out of the huge double gates of Area 1. The stocky guard was still there, right in the middle of putting a fresh wad of dip in his cheek. Walker waved to him and he waved back as he spit into the same bottle and then wiped his fingers on his pant leg.

As they drove back down the dusty, desolate road, Cliff could understand why this was a place to lock up somebody if you wanted them out of the picture. A man could be forgotten in a place like this, sentenced to broil under the Mississippi sun for the rest of his days. It was a place in the world, yet not in it, so far removed from any sign of civilization that it was easy for society to let its existence slip from people's minds. Walker tried not to talk, but he couldn't help but bring up what he had heard.

"He's giving you the same old line. It's a load of crap."

"Well maybe, but I know a little more than I did when I came in here."

"Listen, people on death row don't get too many visitors. He's telling you anything, and I mean anything, just to make himself feel a little sparkle of hope for a few days. He's trying to give himself some reason to think that he might, one day, have even the slimmest chance of getting out of this place. But you and I both know that ain't gonna happen."

"What if his story did have a little truth to it?"

"It doesn't matter. He's staying here till his day comes. No judge ever likes to admit that he sentenced an innocent man to death row. That being the case, they usually just sweep things like that under the rug. Not saying I believe him at all, I'm just saying there ain't no way in hell the State of Mississippi is letting his ass out of here. Once you check into hell, there ain't no checking out."

13

Cliff drove back up the badly maintained highway towards Marks in the silver Expedition. He listened to Vern Gosdin sing *Set 'Em Up Joe* and play Walking the Floor. These Delta radio stations were awesome. They would mix all the good stuff together in one place. The Temptations would be followed by Johnny Cash, an old gospel tune, and then some Barry White.

"That was brother *Vern Gosdin* with a classic!" crowed the DJ excitedly. "This is Ellis Gunnison coming at you out of Mound Bayou, Mississippi. Yeah, y'all know what I'm talking 'bout. Old Mound Bayou, hey! Up next we got a straight toe-tapping, palate-pleasing rendition of *Swing Low Sweet Chariot* from the Ivory Sisters straight out the Big J. That's Jackson, Mississippi y'all! Hey! Hey! This is Ellis Gunnison, proud to be hanging out witcha on ninety-seven point three, y'alls number one resource for the good ole tunes I know ya like!"

Three soulful female voices began to belt the spiritual, and a black Tahoe sped up the road behind Cliff. It didn't attempt to pass, but slowed as it got within ten feet of his back bumper. Up ahead a chip seal county road came to a T with the highway, and a white pickup pulled through the intersection and stopped, blocking both lanes. Cliff tapped his brakes, waiting for the truck to make a move, but it didn't. He came to a stop before he hit the pickup.

Cliff watched in the rearview mirror as the Tahoe turned to block both lanes and it stopped. "Shit, shit, shit," Cliff said to himself. Suddenly two men burst out of the pickup wielding semi-automatic hunting shotguns and ran up to the Expedition, pointing their barrels at Cliff. Two more men with guns came out of the Tahoe behind, surrounding him. Cliff recognized the man directly in front of him through the windshield. It was Arnold Hackworth, Union Cotton's Chief Financial Officer and Sherman's right-hand man. He had a Benelli to his shoulder, aimed a Cliff's head.

Cliff took his hands off the steering wheel. There was a pistol in the glove box but he didn't dare pull it out. One of the men, a big, gruff looking guy, opened Cliff's door and stuck a pistol in his face, "Get out of the car!"

"Alright, easy, easy," said Cliff carefully, and began to slowly get out of the seat. The man stood back and kept the gun pointed at him. When Cliff was completely out of the car, Hackworth pulled the barrel of his shotgun up and propped the weapon across his shoulder. He was wearing sunglasses with blue mirrored lenses.

"Cliff Carver," said Hackworth as he swaggered a little closer. "We're going to take a little ride. We aren't going too far." Then the henchman who had gotten out of the truck with Hackworth slammed the butt of his shotgun into the back of Cliff's right knee and hit him between the shoulder blades with it, knocking him to the ground. Cliff's hands and face slammed against the hot asphalt. The big henchman quickly zip tied Cliff's hands together behind his back, then he grabbed him and hauled him to his feet.

"Let's go," ordered Hackworth. The big henchman grabbed Cliff by the base of the neck and forcefully directed him into the back seat of the pickup truck then slammed the door. Hackworth climbed into the driver's seat and propped his Benelli upright on the floorboard of the passenger side. The big henchman got into the back seat opposite Cliff, his pistol at the ready. Hackworth did a three point turn around and went back down the chip seal road where they had come from.

"What's this about?" demanded Cliff furiously from the backseat.

I don't believe I have to answer that," said Hackworth condescendingly. "You know what this is about. Now, it would seem like you're not in any kind of position to be asking questions. What you need to do is start answering some questions. Who were you going to see down at Parchman today?"

"Somebody that we both know, apparently."

"Let me rephrase that for you smart ass: tell us who you went to talk to or we will blow your face off with some double-ought buckshot and sink your body in a swamp."

"You ought to know him. He used to work with you."

"You didn't know it Cliff, but Clyde Peterman doesn't ever get any visitors. You made a big mistake by going down there today. You shouldn't be sticking your nose in other people's shit, somebody might come up behind you and rub your face in it."

The Expedition and the Tahoe followed in a line behind them. Cliff noticed that there weren't even any power lines running along the side of this road. "How did you know where I was?"

"We have little birds that tell us everything, especially when some dickhead shows up at Parchman asking about Clyde."

"Y'all set him up, didn't you?"

"You can't prove that," Hackworth said, looking into the rearview mirror with an unsettling grin.

"Why'd you do it?"

"Loose lips sink ships. He was too much of an idealist, kinda like you."

"You didn't have the right."

Hackworth snorted, "The right? You must not know much about the way the real world works. It doesn't matter if you have the right, only if you got the pocketbook." Hackworth laughed again, "The right…"

"What about his wife and kids? They haven't seen him since?"

"Hell no, that son of a bitch doesn't even get any phone calls. Besides, nobody in their right mind would bring a good-looking white woman and two little kids for a visit at Parchman."

"Who really killed that hooker?" Cliff asked as he looked at Hackworth's reflection in the rearview mirror.

"Doesn't matter. She's dead now, and Clyde's locked up tight as a tick."

"Who was she, Hackworth? Sure she was a prostitute, but she was just some girl. She had a mama, maybe some kids"

"She was just some nasty bitch off the street from Orange Mound. Nobody would notice much if she was gone, nobody would care. She wasn't even good-looking. Had big ole buck teeth. Disgusting."

Cliff looked out the window, not saying anything. Finally he asked, "Where are you taking me?"

"To do some brotherly bonding. We'll be there in just a minute."

They drove on for another ten minutes, and then turned right and took a dirt road along the edge of a huge field to an old decrepit cotton gin standing in rusty solemnity. The sides were gray sheet metal and the roof was crusted over with thick oxidation. There was an old trailer with tires that had long since rotted off sitting in the weeds beside the building.

Hackworth parked the truck in the dirt and threw his door open. "Alright lets go," he said and grabbed his shotgun. The Expedition and the Tahoe parked behind them. The big henchman walked around the truck and flung Cliff's door open. He reached inside and grabbed Cliff by the shirt.

"I'll get out on my own!" Cliff yelled. He slid out of the truck, hands still zip tied behind him.

"Follow me," said Hackworth.

They walked to the back side of the old gin where there was a set of tall sheet-metal sliding doors set in the wall. One of the henchmen slid the doors open and Cliff felt the hot, stale air from the inside. The light streaming through the open door illuminated a figure, a woman, suspended midair in a tree stand harness used by deer hunters. Her head hung down, her face was bloody, and her eyes were closed. The harness was strapped to a rusty old Hanson cotton scale. It was Leigh.

"Leigh!" Cliff yelled her name and tried to run to her but he was caught and pulled back by two of the henchmen. Leigh looked up slowly and when she saw him her eyes burst open wide. She tried to yell something to him, tried to scream, but the only sounds that came out were muffled shrieks because of the dirty rag jammed into her mouth, held there by a cotton cloth tied around her head. The cloth was stained with blood where the corners of her mouth were. Her hands were bound with zip ties behind her back and her ankles were also zip tied tightly together. Her long gray skirt was torn around the bottom and her white blouse was stained with dirt.

"What have you done to her?" Cliff demanded.

"We haven't done a thing, Cliff. It's your fault she is where she is," derided Hackworth. "Turned her against us, it seems."

"Let her go!" Cliff yelled as he tried to get free.

"Oh we can't do that. She just couldn't quit asking questions. Asked a few too many, and a few of the wrong ones. Was it so she could deliver the answers to you?" asked Hackworth.

"I don't know what you're talking about. She works for you, not for me."

"She's sure been talking to you a whole lot." Hackworth reached down and dug an iPhone out of his pocket with a baby blue case on it. It was hers. He opened up the call log and held the screen up where Cliff could see it. "Look at all these calls."

Cliff said nothing.

"Union Cotton pays the bill for this phone. We know everything that Leigh does on this phone. We also know where she's been because we can track this thing anywhere. Looks like she paid a visit to your office down on Front Street real late at night last Tuesday. Now what was she doing down there?"

"We've been seeing each other but our relationship is strictly personal."

"I find that a bit hard to believe," said Hackworth, "but I am glad you two have found some kind of bond. That's why we are going to play a little game. You're on her team."

He then turned to one of his cronies and said, "Give me the revolver." The man pulled a black six shooter out of a leather holster on his belt and handed it to Hackworth. Hackworth leaned his shotgun up against the wall beside the sliding door. Two of the henchmen still had a tight hold on either side of Cliff.

"What are you doing?" said Cliff.

"You consider yourself a sportsman, don't you?"

"What are you getting at?"

"We are going to try something a little sporting."

He swung out the cylinder of the revolver and knocked all six cartridges out into his hand. He put five of them into his front pocket and kept one out, holding it up between his thumb and his forefinger, a shiny brass .38. He grinned and dropped the cartridge into the cylinder, spun it hard, and then whipped it into place.

"Boy's, y'all get the skeet throwers out, Mr. Carver wants to shoot," said Hackworth excitedly. Two of the men walked out of the gin towards the parked vehicles. "You gonna relax and play nice now? Don't you want to enjoy some gentlemanly fun with us?"

"Get me out of these zip ties, Hackworth."

Hackworth pointed the revolver at Cliff's face and looked down the sights with one eye closed. "You gonna be friendly? We would hate for there to be hostility."

"I'll shoot."

Hackworth pulled the pistol up. "Alright! Y'all cut Cliff's hands free. He's going to put on a little exhibition for us."

The biggest henchman whipped a folding knife out of his pocket and cut the zip ties off Cliff's wrists then let him go. "Walk over here with me Cliff," said Hackworth as he moved towards the doorway. Cliff walked over with angry, resolute strides and stood next to him.

"See, what we are going to do is set up a clay slinger on your left and a slinger on your right. You are going to shoot and hit every one of 'em. Don't you dare miss one either because I'm going to be standing back there and pointing this pistol at Ms. Dalton's pretty little head. Every time you miss, I'm pulling this trigger."

"That's ridiculous."

"Life is that way sometimes, I'm afraid. Let's see how long she can last. Time to put your skills to the test!"

"What if I refuse?"

"Oh you both really won't last long then," Hackworth shook his head with wide, insane eyes.

Cliff crossed his arms calmly and looked out to the cotton field behind the gin. "How many do I have to hit?"

Hackworth shrugged, "Till we run out, I reckon. Hey I got faith in you, Leigh does too."

The two men came back from the Tahoe with the skeet throwers. They were spring-loaded and were operated by placing the clay disk in the throwing arm and pulling the arm back until it locked in place to create tension in the spring. To release it the operator pulls a string, which releases the spring, then the arm whips around and sends the clay flying.

"Y'all set 'em up out there. Cliff is going to stand in the door and shoot that way," said Hackworth, pointing out to the cotton field. The men went to set up the skeet throwers. "That's it. Put 'em about thirty yards apart."

The henchmen went to the Tahoe and came back carrying two boxes of clay pigeons a piece. One of the men had three cases of 12-gauge target loads on top of his two boxes of clays. They walked over to Hackworth, who took the cases of shotgun shells and set them on the ground beside him. "Alright y'all go out there and get ready. Hoooooooo Boy! Mississippi Roulette!" Hackworth eagerly picked up his Benelli and shoved it into Cliff's hands, "Here, gonna need you a fire stick. No funny business now. You don't need to be thinking about anything but hitting them clays." The remaining henchman came up behind Cliff and pointed his shotgun at his head. "Remember, he ain't shooting birdshot like you."

Cliff remained silent. He looked out to the cotton field and shouldered the gun. He looked down the barrel at the orange bead on the end and followed an imaginary clay pigeon through the air. "Only load two shells at a time," said Hackworth. He walked over to Leigh and pointed the revolver at her face. Leigh shrieked and squirmed with everything she had, her eyes wide with fear. "Don't miss!" Hackworth laughed. "She's watching!"

Cliff looked around at the henchman, the end of his shotgun barrel staring him in the face. Cliff swiveled forward and took a deep breath. The cases of cheap Winchester target loads were by his feet. He reached down and opened the first case, took out a box of twenty-five, opened it, and then put two red shells into the Benelli. He pulled the slide back and loaded one shell into the chamber.

Cliff raised the shotgun to his shoulder. He took another deep breath, inhaling and exhaling slowly. "Coming from the right first!" called Hackworth.

"Pull!" shouted Cliff. An orange clay went sailing through the air from the right side. Cliff led it slightly and pulled the trigger. Boom! The disk exploded in midair. "Pull!" Cliff shouted and a clay sailed across from the left. He shot again with the same effect.

"That-a-way! He's deadly!" Hackworth shouted gleefully from behind. "Now it's time for a double! Load 'em up!"

Cliff reached down and loaded two more shells into the gun. He shouldered it and yelled "Pull!" Two clays sailed in from opposite sides. Cliff shot and hit both of them before they crossed each other.

"Impressive!" said Hackworth. "Man you hot today! Load 'em up! Keep the streak going!"

Cliff loaded two more shells. "Pull!" The clay flew through the air and he disintegrated it. "Pull!" He shot and this time the clay splintered along the edge but the main body of it was still intact.

"Ooh! Winged it! Hell, I'll give it to you, we got all day. I'm having fun, aren't you? I know Leigh's having fun!" Hackworth said, and smacked Leigh brutally across her backside. Leigh blasted out an enraged shriek and then some muffled words that would have been a tirade of cussing had her mouth not been full of dirty rag. Cliff grimaced and glared at Hackworth, eyes focused and full of hate.

"Let's go! You got a lot of shooting to do yet!" Hackworth yelled. Cliff loaded two more shells into the gun. He shouldered it, took another deep breath and yelled "Pull!" Two crossing clays came sailing through the air and Cliff nailed both of them. "There we go! The boy is on fire!" yelled Hackworth. Cliff loaded two more shells into the gun.

He waited for the men in the field to load the clay launchers again. He shouldered the gun and yelled "Pull!" He drew a bead on the clay and his finger grew tight on the trigger. The henchman behind him thrust the butt of his shotgun into Cliff's lower back. The Benelli went off and the clay disk fell to the ground, unbroken.

"Oops," grunted the henchman, and stuck the barrel of his gun in Cliff's face as he stood up.

"Damn!" yelled Hackworth. "My turn." He pointed the revolver up at Leigh, who squealed and squirmed, terrified and struggling in futility against the tree stand harness. Hackworth pulled the trigger and the hammer went down with a click. "Shit. It's alright, I missed too. Maybe I'll get her next time. Your turn."

Cliff was boiling. He had to find a way to get out of this. This was madness. He angrily jammed two more shells into the gun and shouldered it. "Do that one again! Pull!" Boom! He busted the clay. "Pull!" Another clay exploded. He loaded two more shells quickly "Pull!"

The two clays went flying through the air but Cliff didn't shoot at them. He ducked down low and in one fluid motion grabbed the barrel of the henchman's shotgun and held it high out of the way. With his other hand, he swung the Benelli around, stuck it in the henchman's gut, and fired. The henchman collapsed onto the ground screaming as blood and mutilated intestine spilled onto the dusty concrete.

The men out in the field were quickly sprinting in his direction. Cliff fired his second shot, dropped the Benelli, picked up the henchman's shotgun, and ducked behind the edge of the doorway. Bullets ripped through the sheet-metal wall to his left. Hackworth was frantically pulling the trigger of the revolver. Click, click, click, pow! It went off and took a chunk out of the floor by Cliff's feet. *Keep moving*, he told himself, *a bird that doesn't fly straight is harder to hit.*

He sprinted behind a big, rusty piece of ginning machinery. Shot pelted the front of the ancient mechanism and Cliff winced sharply. His breathing was brisk and his eyes darted around, searching for options. More bullets pinged into the machine. He stood straight, clutching the gun to his chest.

Cliff slid down to the other end of the machine, a distance of about ten feet, and rapidly glanced around the corner to see the henchmen sprinting towards him. He pulled back and bullets whizzed through the air where his face had just been.

He jumped backwards towards the center of the machine and shouldered the shotgun just as the first henchman came around the corner. Cliff pulled off two brisk, successive cartridges of buckshot that tore into the man's chest and face, leaving behind a splintered, gory, smoking cavern where his mouth once was, and blowing his left shoulder and arm completely off.

Cliff glanced behind him to see the biggest henchman rounding the other side of the machine. He dove to the floor as the big man popped off two pistol rounds, and the shotgun fell out of his hands. Cliff scrambled over the body of the man he had just shot and around the corner of the machine when a bullet nearly shattered his ankle. Hackworth was jamming target loads into the Benelli that Cliff had dropped.

Cliff bolted to his feet and back around the machine, and with a burst of fury, speared the big henchman in the back and tackled him onto the rough concrete. The skin of Cliff's forearm was raked off as the big man's weight landed on it. He intuitively latched his other arm around the man's thick neck. The henchman quickly pushed himself up but Cliff didn't let go, swinging behind him like a cape. Cliff's feet struck the ginning machine and the big henchman roared. Cliff jabbed at his eyes, clawing desperately to make a direct hit. His index finger jammed into one of the eye sockets, impaling the henchman's ocular organ. He screamed in terrible pain as Cliff rotated his finger, mashing the eyeball into a jam of blood and tissue.

Hackworth came speeding around the machine and unloaded a plug of fire that was intended for Cliff but would have undeniably struck them both anyway if Hackworth's birdshot had hit it's correct mark. Instead, the shot poured into the big henchman's chest as he swung Cliff around. Cliff let go and landed on his feet. Hackworth fired his last shell and it struck the henchman's hip as he fell. Cliff heard the clicking of futile trigger pulls.

Cliff gathered all of his strength and vaulted over the big man, crashing into Hackworth and knocking him to the floor. Hackworth struggled to free himself as Cliff punched him in the face repeatedly, yelling intangible curses as loudly as he could. Hackworth held the empty Benelli in his right hand. Cliff snatched it and wielded it with both hands, smashing it down horizontally and mercilessly onto Hackworth's throat, causing some of the blood vessels in his neck to rupture and ooze. Cliff pushed it down with all his weight, as hard as he could, arms shaking from the force they were exerting. He watched his foe's complexion go from red, to violet, and finally to a lifeless white. He stood up and commenced obliterating Hackworth's skull with the butt end of the Benelli until he could no longer stand the utter carnage. He dropped the gun onto the ground, raised his shaking hands into the air, lifted his chin high, and roared at the top of his lungs.

His chest rose and fell mightily. He came back to himself as he brought his face level and scanned the scene of barbaric death surrounding him. Leigh hung there above the floor, her chest beating relentlessly in sheer terror. Cliff walked over and touched her waist. "I'll be right back. I promise I'll be right back." She shrieked and shook violently. "I promise!" He ran over to Hackworth's dead body and rummaged through his pockets for the keys to the pickup truck then ran outside, Leigh's high pitched shrill following him. He let the tailgate down and backed the truck inside the gin.

"Try to lift your feet up!" yelled Cliff out of the window. Leigh squirmed and lifted her bound feet up as high as she could, and Cliff backed the bed of the truck underneath her. She put her feet down on the Rhino-Lining and, for the first time in four hours, the pressure was off of the harness. Cliff got out of the truck, walked back to her, and climbed up in the bed. He pulled out his pocketknife and first cut the cotton strap around Leigh's head. He pulled the wadded up rag out of her mouth and she moved her jaw up and down silently. She didn't speak as Cliff cut the zip ties from her ankles and wrists and helped her out of the tree stand harness. The straps had been cutting off the circulation to her legs, and her underarms ached from hanging there so long.

She trembled as she sat down in the truck bed slowly. Cliff stood by her. "I'm sorry I didn't trust you," he said. Leigh put her forehead on her bent knees with her eyes closed and rocked back and forth. "I'm sorry." He gently touched her back and she swatted his hand away forcefully. "We can't stay here," said Cliff. "We have to go." She continued to rock with her head down. "We have to leave, now," Cliff pleaded. "Look at me. Leigh, look at me!" he touched her again and she shivered all over and rubbed her forehead into her knees. "Leigh, please!"

She looked up with agonized red eyes, trembling lips, and a quivering nose. Her gaze told Cliff that she had been frightened more than she ever thought possible—hurt like no one should ever be hurt—like something in her soul had been ripped out. Cliff squatted down, "Leigh, we have to go. Come on please." His eyes started to well up. "Leigh…" A tear fell, he didn't have the words. He stood back up and grabbed her hand, and she stood up dejectedly. He dropped down and helped her off the tailgate, then led her by the hand to the Expedition outside.

He opened the door for her and helped her in. "I've got to go hide the other vehicle," he said. "Wait here." She looked back at him blankly. He shut the door, went to get the Tahoe keys out of the dead henchman's pocket, pulled the Tahoe into the gin, and slid the doors closed as he walked out. Cliff started the Expedition and pulled away down the dirt road through the field. Leigh looked straight ahead with empty eyes. He turned back onto the paved road.

Leigh began to cry. She cried like she would never stop as they drove and Cliff didn't attempt to get her to calm down. She wailed and snotted all over herself. After ten minutes Cliff asked cautiously, "They didn't do anything to you down there, did they?"

She shook her head no.

"What happened?"

"They told me they wanted me to go meet a landowner with Hackworth," she sniveled. "I got in his truck and we drove down here." Another wail burst from her. "When we pulled up, all those men were there and they pulled me out of the truck and hit me on the face. Then they tried to gag me and shove that harness around me. I struggled and kicked and one of them stomped on me. I tried to get up, tried to run away." She looked out of the window and sucked some painful gulps of air. "They held me down with a knife to my throat and told me to be still. I was so scared." The tears flowed. "Then they forced that harness on me and hung me up in there. I thought I was going to die."

"I'm so sorry Leigh," Cliff pleaded. "I'm such an idiot. I should've trusted you."

She continued to weep and looked blankly out the window.

"This wouldn't have happened to you if it weren't for me," he shook his head in painful remorse, looking ahead with both hands on the wheel. "We can't go home."

She sniffed and turned to look at him. "Where are you taking me?"

"To a hospital first. After that, I know a place we can go where you'll be safe."

14

The next morning, Cliff woke up in one of Brevard Pope's guest bedrooms. He dressed and went into the room next to his where Leigh was sleeping. He reached down and stroked her hair. She had stitches in the corner of her mouth and scrapes and bruises all over her, including a big, deep bruise on the back of her thigh where she had been stomped on. Late the night before, he had helped her gently into bed and she was asleep by the time her head hit the pillow. She had on a pair of Nike running shorts and a t-shirt that Cliff had bought for her to put on while she was at the hospital. He kissed her on the top of her head and went downstairs, where Brevard Pope was sipping coffee in the kitchen of his impressive antebellum manse.

"Morning Mr. Pope," he said wearily as he entered the room.

"Good Morning!" Pope returned vibrantly. "How's our angelic house guest doing?"

"She's still asleep. I'm afraid it's going to take her a while," Cliff said, worried.

"She's in good hands. My wife and I will do everything in our power to see to it that she makes a full recovery. Would you like a cup of coffee?"

"That'd be great."

Pope got up and poured Cliff a cup and handed it to him. His face turned serious and concerned. His mouth went into a straight line and his brows hugged the rims of his eye sockets tighter. "What have you gotten yourself into, Cliff? Why where those men after y'all? We're alone, tell me the truth."

Cliff breathed out and crimped his lips. "I don't know if I'm supposed to tell you."

"Cliff it's me, come on. My lips are sealed. I just don't want you getting in any more scrapes. Kenny would want me to look after you."

Cliff gazed down and to the side, put his coffee cup on the counter, and crossed his arms. He knew Brevard only wanted to help, having the best intentions in mind. Zoey would destroy him if he told anybody, but Brevard wasn't just anybody. He looked back up apprehensively and said, "Alright. I'm dead serious, you can't tell anybody, not even your wife. I'm working as an informant with the federal government. There is an investigation going on with the intention of taking down Union Cotton and Walton Sherman. They convinced me to leverage my position as a landowner to uncover information."

Pope looked back at him with surprise and concern. "Your position is very dangerous, that's what your position is! Cliff, be reasonable. You haven't done anything wrong, have you? They can't force you to continue. You need to be thinking about McIntyre Trading."

Cliff's emotions were confused. He knew Pope was right in one sense, but was all this for nothing? Mr. Kenny, his house, Leigh, all of it? It couldn't be. He couldn't quit now. "I've got to keep going, Mr. Pope. Walton Sherman killed Mr. Kenny," said Cliff.

Pope's face convoluted into perplexed, sad, and angry at the same time. He looked away and sat down at the kitchen table, attempting to absorb the news that it was indeed murder. "I had thought that myself but I didn't want to believe it. I was afraid that if I said it out loud it would make it true." He stared at the table, not really seeing it, but instead seeing his friend's face. "Is there anything I can do?"

"You can take care of Leigh and make sure that no one finds her. I'm worried about her."

"We will. We'll treat her like one of our own."

"You're a history professor… do you know anything about the Gayoso Hotel?" Cliff asked on a whim.

"Oh yes, The Gayoso was the most luxurious place in Memphis at one time. It was one of the first places in the city to have running water. That hotel was the focal point of high society when Memphis was younger. Why do you ask?"

"Someone told me that Sherman owns the old Gayoso Hotel building in downtown."

"That building is actually the second incarnation of the Gayoso Hotel," Pope informed him. "The original burned around the turn of the twentieth century."

"I didn't even know about it. I've never really heard anybody talk about it before."

"The Gayoso Hotel was almost as old as the city herself. It served as the headquarters of the Union Army when they occupied Memphis during the Civil War. While the war was going on there was an embargo on trading with the South, and that place was the epicenter of the cotton black market," Pope said, embellishing the words with intrigue. "Some of the Union officers stationed there made a lot of money taking kickbacks from the illegal cotton trade."

Cliff pooched a quizzical frown. "Was William Tecumsah Sherman ever stationed there?"

"He was the commanding officer there for a while before he went to fight in Georgia," replied Pope. "That's an awfully specific question."

"William Tecumseh Sherman is Walton Sherman's great-great grandfather."

"Oh I see," Pope sat back thinking. "So the family fortune might have been ill-gained is what you're saying."

"Maybe so. Maybe he handpicked some land around here that he wanted to buy. Union Cotton was started with land passed all the way down from the general."

"Or confiscated by the general," added Pope.

"Hey, do something for me. This stays between you and me, too. Find out everything you can about the wreck of the SS *Sultana*." Cliff wasn't going to tell Zoey about the shipwreck. Clyde was right, as crazy as he might have seemed, the government might try to kill off any excavation project. It was eating at his curiosity and he wanted to find out a little more for himself.

"The *Sultana* sank right out there in the river just upstream from downtown," Pope replied.

"See if you can figure out where it sank exactly," Cliff said. "I think it might have something to do with why Sherman wants that place so bad."

"OK? And why's that?"

"I went to Parchman yesterday," began Cliff.

Pope spat some of his coffee. "You went to Parchman! That's not a good place to be hanging out Cliff."

"I know, I know, just hear me out," Cliff raised his hands in caution. "I talked to a guy in there who used to work for Sherman. He said that Sherman was convinced that the *Sultana* had a lot of gold on board when it sank and he wanted to use the hunting land as base for a secret excavation attempt. It sounds crazy, but it's going to bother me until I know. Help me disprove it."

Pope looked at him skeptically. "Sounds like that guy was a nut. It was carrying Union troops home when it sank."

"Just try. See what you can find. It would help me out. And see what you can find out about Clyde Peterman. He's the guy I talked to down there. He's on death row for murdering a hooker in a Byhalia motel room but he swears that Sherman framed him. Try pulling his case records or something."

"Well alright," Pope acquiesced, "I'll see what I can do."

•••

Cliff met Zoey and Marvin at the FBI office later that day. They stood around Marvin's cubicle as he typed away and Zoey fumed. "It's fucking serious now! Nobody else gets hurt. I won't be having any more casualties under my watch. That son of a bitch is getting what's coming to him."

"Avalon Bullion and Rare Collectibles," read Marvin from the screen.

"It says they have a history of releasing previously undocumented gold and silver coins."

"Are they fakes?" asked Zoey.

Marvin shook his head, "From what the database is telling me, they're undeniably authentic. Some of them have sold for hundreds of thousands of dollars. They cater to the world's wealthiest collectors."

"So what's the deal?" asked Zoey. "Does Sherman own a part of it?"

"No," Marvin shook his head and kept reading.

"What else did that Peterman guy have to say?" asked Zoey.

Cliff was leaning against the side of the cubicle. "He said that Sherman was always flying to New York to meet with this Avalon group and that he bought that building downtown to build a vault in the basement because he likes to collect rare coins and jewels and stuff. Peterman also said that Sherman framed him because he found out that he was trying to kill Ronny Millwood a couple of years ago."

"He didn't give any indication as to what Sherman's motive might have been?"

Cliff crimped his lips together and shook his head, "Nope."

"What the hell is he using that land for?" Zoey said, more to herself than to anybody.

Marvin perked up excitedly, "Holy shit. I think that's it."

"What?" asked Zoey.

Marvin spun around. "That's where the money is coming from for the Gayoso Fund. Most of the wire transfers going into the fund originate somewhere around New York. I'd bet they're coming from this Avalon Bullion place. You should go up there."

"Alright we'll check it out," said Zoey. "In the meantime, get a search warrant for the Gayoso apartment building. Cliff, you're coming with me."

15

Cliff and Zoey walked up the busy Manhattan sidewalk to a gray granite building with a heavy oak door, a golden awning, and brightly illuminated windows filled with gold and silver bullion coins. AVALON BULLION & RARE COLLECTIBLES was etched into the front door. They pulled the door open and walked inside, where they were greeted by a well groomed man wearing small round glasses and a slim-fitting suit with no tie. He extended his hands graciously. "Welcome, are you looking for something particular today?" he asked in a British accent.

"No," Cliff said. "Just browsing, thank you. Aren't we, dear?" he turned to Zoey and smiled.

"Oh yes darling, just browsing." She grabbed Cliff's hand and winked at the salesman, as if she was determined to walk out of there with something.

Cliff and Zoey walked around the sparkling room. Rows upon rows of glass cases lined the walls, all filled with shining gold and silver coins and bars of different sizes and weights. Cliff had never seen anything like it before. There were South African Krugerrands, Canadian Maple Leafs, Chinese Pandas, UK gold sovereigns, ingots from Australia's Perth Mint, and United States silver dollars. *Who had the money to come in here and casually pick up a few gold coins?* Cliff wondered to himself. Zoey inspected the cases lustily. Cliff looked even harder.

He spied several Double Eagles in a case. "Can I have a magnifying glass or something?" Cliff asked.

"Certainly, sir. I'll bring one and open the case for you," replied the salesman. He came walking over with an ivory-handled magnifying glass set in a gold rim. Cliff was almost afraid to use it for fear that he would drop it and have to pay for it. Zoey wasn't going to pay that shit. The man opened up the case and Cliff carefully studied the dates on each coin. He realized that the one he was looking for wasn't there.

"Do you have any Double Eagles from 1865?" he asked.

"No sir, that's a very rare year."

Cliff looked back at him calmly and unblinking for a few seconds, and then his mouth formed a half smirk. "What about in the money room?" he asked, sounding very secretive.

The salesman gasped, "You mean the private client foy-yay?"

"Yes," Cliff said. "Take us there."

"Yes, sir. Only the most discerning collectors are even aware of its existence," the salesman grinned.

Zoey smiled at Cliff without showing any teeth and popped her eyebrows up and back down quickly. She was impressed by his intuition. The salesman led them through a door in the back of the room, up a flight of stairs, and down a long hall, then took a large golden skeleton key out of his inside jacket pocket and unlocked the heavy door at the end of the hall. He opened the door to reveal a gleaming treasure room that sparkled brightly underneath can lights set in the aluminum tile ceiling. "Oh!" Zoey gasped in giddy excitement. The man stepped inside, held the door for them, and swung his arm out in welcome. "Ma'am and sir, the private client foy-yay," he said slowly, building anticipation.

They stepped in eagerly, and *it was* a breathtaking sight to behold. A small golden idol from a long lost South American civilization stared back them ruthlessly from a shelf behind a pane of glass. There was a golden Spanish cross, Spanish doubloons, and coins from the Roman Empire, Babylon, and ancient Ethiopia. Cliff and Zoey spun around, astounded. "This is incredible," exclaimed Cliff.

"Thank you sir," replied the salesman. "We only show this to our most valuable clientele."

Cliff walked around the room wide-eyed, examining the pieces, and then he saw one—an 1865 Double Eagle. Wait. He looked harder. There were three of them in a row. "Where did you get these?" Cliff asked.

"We get them from a private collector," replied the salesman.

"Can I see them?"

"Absolutely sir," said the salesman, and unlocked the case. "These are in pristine condition and from your favored year, 1865. They were minted at Philadelphia. Very rare." He pulled a white glove out of his pocket and picked one of them up. He held it up so Cliff could look at it closely. "As you'll notice, the words 'In God We Trust' are absent."

"I see that," said Cliff.

"This was the last year that the United States minted series one of the Double Eagle. The next year they began series two, which saw the addition of the now-standard phrase on its face."

Cliff looked the coin over studiously. "I like these pieces."

"They are very valuable sir, a wise addition to any discerning collection," returned the salesman.

Cliff asked the question that he and Zoey had rehearsed earlier. "I'm a very private man," he said evenly. "Will my transaction be recorded?"

"No sir, we provide all of our private clients with the utmost secrecy. All of our private client transactions are anonymous."

"You don't keep records?" asked Cliff as if it were more of a prerequisite for purchase than an actual question.

"No sir, never for the money room, as you called it."

"Hold it!" yelled Zoey. "FBI. You're under arrest." She held her badge up and the man's jaw dropped fearfully. "You don't keep records? What about antiquities law? Is all this black market stuff?" The salesman held his hands up and stammered. "We'll search this place up and down, so tell us right now where you keep the ledgers," demanded Zoey.

"Ma'am, I'm sorry but I can't give you any," sputtered the salesman nervously. "The records for this room don't exist."

"They don't exist anywhere?" she prodded.

"No. Our private clients are very…" he looked down and thought about what he was about to say because he realized how it would come across. "Please forgive me, but they are very private. The actual buyers and sellers never meet each other; this is just a showroom where we handle the transactions for them."

"Oh, okay," Zoey drew out. "But you see the buyers and the sellers, don't you?"

"Yes, I do."

"And you know them very well? Their tastes, what they like, what they're on the lookout for?"

"Yes. That's the most important part of the personalized service that I provide. That's why they trust me with these items of great value."

"So you know Walton Sherman, then," Cliff suggested.

The man looked at Cliff and his face tensed, the skin of his nose drew up, and he looked back with immobile eyes. "I've never heard that name before."

"Then how are you getting these 1865 Double Eagles?"

The salesman broke eye contact and looked back at Zoey, hands still raised. "I'm not at liberty to say."

"You're not going to be at liberty to do anything if you don't cooperate!" ejected Zoey. "Who do you get them from?"

The salesman's eyes darted back and forth between Zoey and Cliff. "Please, don't make me answer that question," his voice quivered. "The best I can do is to tell you that they're from a private collector."

"WHO!?" Zoey demanded.

"I won't spend the rest of my life in a goddamn witness protection program!" cried the salesman desperately.

"Then tell us where the money from the sale of these Double Eagles goes," Cliff demanded.

"I can't recall." The salesman looked at the floor.

"Is the money deposited into the Gayoso fund?" interrogated Zoey.

The salesman's eyes got wide and he breathed sharply through his mouth. "Like I said, the records don't exist."

"Hand's behind your back," Zoey commanded, and cuffed him. She drew her phone out of her pocket and held it to her ear. "Marv, it's Zoey. Send somebody to arrest Sherman and freeze all of his accounts. I think we got enough to get him to confess. Do it quick." She hung up. "Let's go." She grabbed the salesman and directed him out of the room and down the stairs.

Cliff followed behind them, and as he did he received a text message.

BREVARD POPE: Come to my house. I got something that you need to see.

16

Cliff and Zoey flew back to Memphis and landed that evening. When they got to the office Marvin was sweating bullets. He turned around in his chair to face them as they walked up, his face red and anxiety-stricken. "Sherman's gone."

Zoey clenched her fists by her side tightly and gritted her teeth. "What do you mean he's gone?" she asked slowly.

"We can't find him."

"FUCK! DAMN IT!" Zoey ripped Marvin's Batman calendar off the wall and threw it across the room. Everyone there had immediately turned sharply and was looking at her. She slammed her fists violently on Marvin's desk repeatedly. She stopped, leaned on her clenched fists, and looked over at Marvin. "If he gets out of the country we're fucked." She rubbed her forehead. "Find that son of a bitch! I don't care what we got to do. We've been working on this too long. Find him! Put out a warrant for all the politicians that took his bribe. Maybe one of those fuckers will know where he is."

Cliff was a little frightened by Zoey's behavior. She had never shown this side around him before. He backed up a little bit. "So, what do you want me to do?" he asked.

Zoey rubbed her eyes, "I don't fucking care." She flipped the back of her hand at him without looking. "Take the night off. Go to the zoo. Get some fucking ice cream or something."

"O...kay," Cliff backed out of the cubicle slowly. "Call me if you need me." Zoey didn't look at him. Marvin did, and he looked worried.

•••

Cliff drove the Expedition down Brevard Pope's oak-lined driveway and his white-columned mansion stood in charming dignity at the end. The driveway formed a circle in front of the house; Cliff parked on the side and walked up onto the portico and knocked on the door. A black lab came running around the house wagging his tail excitedly and Cliff patted him on the head. A few seconds later, Pope swung the door open and welcomed him. "Hello Sport! Come on in. I see you've met Augustus," he said, referring to the dog.

"Hey Mr. Pope." He stepped into a beautiful central hallway that he hadn't spent any time paying attention to the first time he was here.

"No, Augustus," said Pope. "Stay outside." He closed the door.

There was no furniture, and no pictures hung from the walls lest they should cover up the plaster that served as the canvas for a beautiful floor-to-ceiling mural on both sides. On one side there were scenes of Kentucky flatboats poling along a riverbank, boys fishing with cane poles, and a Sunday dinner on the ground outside of a white wooden church. On the other side was a swamp with toothy, grinning alligators, a plantation ball with southern belles in colorful dresses, and a group of men hunting with their pointer dogs flushing up a covey of quail close by. "You know, I didn't tell you before, but this hallway is something else," he said, looking around appreciatively.

"You like that? As you walk down the hall it's supposed to be like you're taking a steamboat trip on the Mississippi River during the early eighteen hundreds. My grandmother commissioned an artist from Nashville to paint the hallway like this back in the twenties. She had been going to Nashville a lot from what I've heard." Pope looked around at the scenes on the wall. "He lived here with them while he painted it. It took him the better part of two years. One of the many family eccentricities."

"It's so detailed. I can tell he put a lot of time in it."

"Yeah, he was putting into my grandmother a lot too, I think."

Cliff laughed. That was the last thing he expected Brevard Pope to say. "What?"

"We suspect they were having an affair. Whenever somebody in the family does something stupid we say that they must be related to the artist," Pope grinned mischievously.

Cliff laughed. "That's funny. Where's Leigh?"

At that moment, Leigh came walking into the hallway in a white cotton dress.

Pope turned around. "There she is." He gave a fatherly smile. "And feeling a little better."

Cliff met her halfway down the central hall. "Hi." They didn't touch. He looked into her eyes and she looked back into his. The stitches in her mouth were still pretty fresh but she was looking better.

"Hey," she returned.

"How do you feel?"

"I feel alright."

"Do you like staying here?" he smiled and looked around.

She smiled back delicately. "It's beautiful. I love it."

"I thought to myself that you might like this place. Will you go sit in the garden with me later?" His eyes pleaded for forgiveness and to rekindle something real that he now felt like an idiot for trying to suppress. She looked at him like she wanted to but wasn't sure how.

"Yes," she said.

"Cliff, you want to come upstairs for a minute?" asked Mr. Pope, sensing that it was time for an interjection.

Cliff looked over his shoulder, "Yeah." He looked back into Leigh's eyes and then turned around and followed Pope up the stairs.

"This is my favorite room in the house," said Pope as he flipped on the lights to a big room on the left side of the hall. Tall windows dominated the exterior walls and there were floor-to-ceiling bookshelves lining the inside of the room. In the exact center of the outer wall was the mounted head of a bull elk, its antlers stretching to the ceiling. Underneath the elk was an antique globe in a wooden cradle. "Come sit with me." Pope sat down in front of a laptop computer at a wooden oval table in the center of the room and Cliff sat beside him.

"What'd you find out?" Cliff asked.

"It seems that Marshall County, Mississippi no longer has any information from Clyde Peterman's case. They say that the court records were lost shortly after the case was over." said Pope with a smirk.

"Huh. Not surprised. Did you find anything at all about him?"

"No, not particularly. All I did was become more convinced that he is innocent. I was able to find a few old articles about the case from the Commercial Appeal, but it seems as if everything else about it has vanished into thin air."

"Seems to confirm Peterman's story."

"That's my thinking, too."

"What about the boat?" asked Cliff.

Pope leaned back farther in his chair. "Now *that* I can tell you about. The *Sultana* was a sidewheeler paddle boat that operated before and during the Civil War. She was one of largest and most grand old dames of her day. Towards the end of her life she carried passengers and cargo between New Orleans and St. Louis. The captain was a man by the name of J.C. Mason, a St. Louis resident with Southern sympathies.

He, along with some other investors, bought the *Sultana* and used her during the war. They seem to have tried their best to stay out of the mess of the fighting because records show that they ran the river pretty much all the way through the course of the war. Of course, when the Union Army gained complete control of the river again, Yankee military contracts were quite lucrative and I imagine they took full advantage of that.

At the end of the war, she sank in the Mississippi about four miles north of downtown Memphis. On her last journey, she was carrying Union soldiers who had been POWs at the Confederate prison camps at Cahaba and Andersonville back to Illinois so they could find their way home. The boat was terribly overloaded, bursting at the seams with all the men that were crammed on it. On the night of April 27, 1865, a huge explosion rocked the ship, killing most everybody onboard, including the captain. It was the largest maritime disaster in the history of the United States. More people died on the *Sultana* than on the *Titanic*."

"Really?" said Cliff in disbelief. "Then how come I haven't ever heard of it?"

"It took place only a week or so after the assassination of President Lincoln," continued Pope. "News didn't travel as fast at that time and chances are, when the boat sank, many people were just learning about the assassination. Lincoln's death and the manhunt afterwards for John Wilkes Booth trumped any other news that was going on at the time. The accident got minimal press coverage because the papers were all using their resources to cover the Lincoln story."

Cliff drummed his fingers on the top of the table for a few moments. "You said the ship blew up?"

"More or less," said Pope. "The boiler exploded. Some people say that it was a hotspot in the boiler that caused the explosion." He brought his hands up to illustrate what he was about to say. "When the ship was listing back and forth under the extra weight on its trip upstream, the water in the boiler would slosh from one side to the other. This would result in a small section of the boiler being dry for a short period of time. Without any water on top of the metal to absorb the heat, the metal in that spot would bubble, and if it happened enough, and the same spot got enough heat, it would burst. The built-up pressure trying to escape the boiler would then have caused the explosion." Pope paused. "But some people don't think that's what happened."

"What do they say?" asked Cliff.

"They say that the explosion was no accident. Some people believe that somebody planted a coal bomb on board."

"A coal bomb?"

"A piece of metal, cast to look like a lump of coal, filled with gunpowder and then rolled in coal dust so it wouldn't look any different than the rest of the coal in the pile," said Pope.

"Then somebody would put it in the coal pile, and then they would unknowingly shovel it into the boiler, right?" said Cliff.

"You got it. There were even some people who came forward and claimed to have been the one who planted the bomb. Ex-Confederates mostly, but most people just dismissed them as crazies looking for their fifteen minutes of fame." Cliff could tell that Pope had something else on his mind.

"What do you think happened to it?" he asked.

"Pull your chair here a bit closer. I want you to see the computer," said Pope. Cliff got out of his seat, picked it up by the backrest and moved in closer to Pope. He sat down again where he could more comfortably view the computer screen. Pope flipped the screen up, turned the computer on, and went into the files on the computer's hard drive and opened one up.

When the file opened, what looked like a great, twisting snake appeared on the screen. The snake's body was bright green, and the area surrounding it was black with white lines running across it at different angles and intersecting at irregular places. "Do you know what that is?" asked Pope.

"No."

"That's the Mississippi River as it was in 1865. This is the section of the river one hundred miles upstream and downstream from Memphis. Those lines mark state boundaries and county lines as they were in 1865. See, Memphis is marked on the map," said Pope, and pointed to a dot just right of center on the screen.

"OK, I see it."

"Now look at this X," said Pope, pointing to a spot in the river about a half an inch above the dot on the screen. "That's where the records indicate the *Sultana* sank. Now watch this."

Pope tapped the enter key and suddenly the river came to life, slithering this way and that way, doubling back on itself, and writhing in an uncontrolled manner. This continued for a few minutes. "What we are watching," explained Pope, "is the process scientists call helicoidal flow. It is the constant process of water pushing against its banks, eroding areas, forming loops and bends, and then doubling back on itself, breaking through, and forming a new channel. You ever heard of an oxbow lake?"

"Yeah."

"That's how oxbow lakes are formed; they are old loops in the river that are left behind when the river breaks through to a new channel. Water will always take the path of least resistance. The Mississippi River is a living, breathing thing, constantly changing."

"Man this is cool," Cliff proclaimed.

"We are taking a trip through time. It will calm down in just a second when the timeline hits about the thirties. That's when the Army Corps of Engineers really started to bulk up their efforts to straighten it out and keep it more predictable for improved navigation. That's when the river really became the modern waterway we know today. The county lines change too, especially right after the Civil War. The Reconstruction state governments changed the way a lot of the counties were drawn up. Created some new counties out of old ones and reshaped others."

Sure enough, soon the writhing snake of the river began to calm down and seemed to stay in the same place, or at least move more slowly. When the timeline at the bottom of the screen came to an end, the simulation stopped. "Now, this is where the river is today," said Pope. "Notice anything different?"

Cliff pointed to the X that marked the wreck of the *Sultana*. "The X isn't in the river anymore."

"That's right." said Pope and then zoomed in closer to the X on the screen. "The river channel along that stretch is actually two miles to the east of where it was in 1865. We are zoomed in on Crittenden County, Arkansas."

Cliff inspected the screen harder. "That's the farmland Mr. Kenny bought," said Cliff in a state of disbelief. "That's where it is. The X is sitting on top of the duck club."

"Or underneath it, you mean," added Pope.

"It's there? The *Sultana* is really there? Underneath the ground?"

"By my illustration it would appear to be that way. Covered up by years of sediment, probably underneath a soybean field."

"That's wild," said Cliff, trying to absorb this new information. "How did you figure this out?"

"I've still got some skills left from my days as a geologist in the oil industry," smiled Pope. "Never thought I'd be doing this again."

Cliff looked back at the screen as if he had to check one more time to make sure the X was in the same place. "Peterman is turning out to be half right," he said, stunned. "That's why Sherman killed Mr. Kenny."

"What do you propose we do?" asked Pope.

"I have no idea." His jaw was slack. He closed his mouth and looked at Pope excitedly as he anticipated their next move. "We should dig for it ourselves!" He jabbed Pope on the arm.

Pope nodded slowly, "We should get some professionals involved, university archaeologists. They would be all over this and they would know how to go about it better than I do."

"No. We don't want to do anything that will draw attention."

"Why is that?"

"Couldn't the government confiscate anything we found? I want to keep it."

"Cliff," Pope chastised. "Any artifacts we find belong in a museum. They belong to the American people. There are laws for that kind of thing, too. If there is some gold onboard I don't think they would take every last penny's worth. I'm sure they'd let us keep a souvenir or two for our trouble."

"Yeah." Now Cliff felt a little ashamed. "Yeah, you're right. I think we should wait, though. If we told anybody and they went out there and started looking around and Sherman found out, it could put them in danger."

"Well they're going to arrest him soon, aren't they?" asked Pope.

"They don't know where he is. He's gone AWOL."

"What?" Pope said in shock. "He's missing?"

"Yeah. They're afraid he might've gotten wise and left the country."

"As long as he's out of the country and not around here. He wouldn't have a way of finding out that Leigh is staying with us, would he?"

Cliff shook his head, "Nah, y'all are fine, don't worry. He's running from the long arm of the law. He's probably at a beach house in Thailand, or in his secret lair in the middle of a volcano, or something ridiculous."

Pope huffed a dismissive laugh. "I sure hope so. You ought to go downstairs and talk to that girl. I think she likes you."

"You know what, I'm going to do that. Mr. Pope, you're awesome. Thank you so much."

"Not a problem sport, be suave," he winked.

Cliff walked downstairs, trying to fight back his nerves. He walked into the living room and she wasn't there. He walked across the hall to the kitchen and still she wasn't there. "Leigh?" he called. Cliff walked back into the central frescoed hallway. He turned around, trying to decide where she might've gone, and then opened the back door.

Leigh was sitting on the back steps in the dark by herself, holding a blanket in her lap. She looked up as Cliff opened the door. "Hey," he said. She didn't say anything, but held out her hand. Cliff took it, and she stood up while looking back at him longingly, silently. She led him through the Pope's perfectly symmetrical flower garden beneath the light of the moon and through the grass to the edge of a large, recently harvested cornfield. She let go of his hand and spread the blanket out on the ground. She stepped closer to him, gently touching his face with her fingers, and inhaled close to his neck, moving slowly, gracefully and mysteriously. Her lips gently touched his neck in a moist kiss and she grabbed his hand again, gazing into his eyes like she could see right into his soul, and beckoned him to sit with her.

They sat cross-legged on the blanket together, and Leigh grabbed Cliff's upper left arm with both hands and leaned into him, letting her weight rest on his shoulder. Her head nuzzled just underneath his. Cliff looked over at her. She was incredibly beautiful—her hair more curly than usual—in the white dress, stitches and all. He could feel her chest gently moving in and out, communicating a trust that didn't need to be articulated. They sat in the dark silently. Cliff moved his head over to touch the top of hers.

"It's not your fault," she said quietly.

"I feel like it is," he returned.

"It's not your fault."

"You're strong."

"You're brave."

"You're beautiful."

"You're gallant."

"You're intelligent."

"You're heroic."

"You're captivating."

"You're the man I want to be with."

Cliff lifted his head up and looked at her. She was gorgeous. Her face, her body, her mind. He took his free hand and gently touched her chin. She turned to look at him and he kissed her tenderly on the side of her mouth without stitches. She looked into his eyes with a longing passion and Cliff reciprocated it back to her. She turned her face and rubbed her cheek against his, closing her eyes. Cliff did the same, instinctively responding to her subtle movements.

Thwack. Cliff felt like he had just gotten stung in the arm by a really big bee. He looked over aggravated, and saw the dart sticking into his skin. "What the…" His head began to spin and he teetered back and forth. "Cliff? Cliff what's wrong?" questioned Leigh anxiously. He wasn't coherent enough to respond. His vision faded and he fell comatose onto the blanket.

17

Cliff blinked a few times and began to come to his senses. His head bobbed around on his neck and then he stretched his chin up into the air with his eyes closed. He squeezed out a high-pitched grunt and realized that he was sitting in a chair upright. He tried to move his arms but couldn't, and felt the cord digging into his wrists. He looked out with blurry vision and saw fuzzy blobs. He squeezed his eyelids together tightly for five seconds and opened them back up.

He was in a tan living room filled with duck mounts and fake leather furniture. He fought to move again, his wrists and feet bound to the chair. He began to panic and howled as he shook back and forth, violently attempting to break free. He yelled and gyrated in the chair, flexing his muscles and doing everything that he could to wrest himself from the bindings. He fell over with the chair and his head smacked into the floor. He inhaled sporadically through his nose and continued to struggle as the panic drove on. Cliff heard the creaking of springs from a recliner and somebody standing up. He stopped moving. They walked behind him and grabbed the rungs on the back of the chair, lifting him effortlessly and setting him upright. A few footsteps, and Walton Sherman appeared in front of him.

"Glad you're finally awake." Sherman smacked Cliff hard and open-handed across the face. Cliff cringed and wiggled his jaw back and forth slowly a few times and glared at Sherman hatefully. Sherman had on an expensive suit, his hair was combed meticulously, and his face was smooth as a polished marble statue. Sherman brought his face within inches of Cliff's.

"You just won't go away, will you?" Cliff squinted and jerked his face back. Sherman's breath smelled strongly of Listerine.

Sherman stared at Cliff with eyes that were blue and cold and hard. "What's the point?" he asked. "Think about your life. What it could've been. What do you see?" Cliff stared back at him without speaking. "You're not even going to voice yourself?" asked Sherman pityingly. "Be proud! You're Cliff fucking Carver! Come on, what do you see?"

"I see myself out of this damn chair," said Cliff coldly.

"Oh I know you can do better than that. Think about all you could've had, the life that you could've lived. Is there a nice brick home? A petite little wife and two kids who run and hug you when you get home from work? Are you grilling steaks with the neighbors on the weekends? Do you have a lake house on Pickwick? Sounds pretty good, doesn't it?"

"Where am I?" Cliff asked defiantly.

"We'll get there, don't you worry. Cliff you could've lived a good life. Hell, I did you a favor and made you boss of that outfit over there. You had everything going for you—why stand in my way over one little piece of ground?"

"You didn't do me a favor. You're a murderer."

Sherman stood up and laughed and shook his head, how stupid. "Cliff you have no idea. Who do you think runs the world? Kindergarten teachers and car salesmen?" he spat. "That's what makes men powerful. It's not the ability to kill, we all have the capacity to kill, it is the will to do what is necessary. We're all animals, all of us," he shook his head in ethereal amusement. "It doesn't matter how civilized you think you are, how educated, how refined. We're all just a bunch of animals. We all fuck, we all consume, we all kill. It's natural selection."

Cliff held his head up. "If that's how you see the world, you must really be an animal."

"We all are, but we let our emotions make us stupid," Sherman chastised. "Emotions serve no practical purpose in the modern world. We are struggling against ten thousand years of evolution in an environment that has really only existed for less than one hundred years. The two things that really matter are what we can do, and what we will do. The ones that have the will are the ones who make the rules."

"Where's Leigh?" Cliff asked, not amused by Sherman's monologue.

Sherman formed a twisted grin, "She's perfectly safe." He began to chuckle. "You really thought she was in love with you!" He doubled over in laughter. "She told me where you were. Another example of how emotions make us weak."

Cliff's heart sank and he felt like someone had rammed a hot blade through his chest. He looked at the floor. There was no way. No. No, she wouldn't. He closed his eyes in overwhelming pain. She couldn't, not after everything. The intense, white hot agony seared through his heart.

"You seem to have forgotten that she works for me," exclaimed Sherman cheerfully.

"What about Hackworth?"

"Fuck him, finance guys are a dime a dozen. Although, I have to say that I'm impressed with the body count you're stacking up. You might've had more will in you than you realize. Who are you to point the finger?"

"They were all working for you," said Cliff, astounded.

Sherman brought his palm to his heart. "Oh I know," he said with sarcastic empathy. "I'm going to have to get you back for that." He delivered another blow across Cliff's face. Cliff inhaled angrily and turned his head back towards Sherman, glowering furiously at him.

"You want to know where you are?" said Sherman. "I'll tell you. The land that you're about to sign over to me starts right across the road. Welcome to the High Cotton Duck Club, Cliff." Sherman extended his arms wide. "I hate it for your sake that you aren't here on a happier errand, but that land is mine one way or another."

Cliff took a deep breath, fighting back the pain of Leigh's betrayal. "What's on the *Sultana*?"

Sherman's eyes got wide like he was surprised, and then he grinned. "Very good Cliff. Well I guess there's no harm in telling you since this will probably be your last day on this earth. The *Sultana* has kept the origin of my family's fortune a secret since the Civil War. I intend for it to remain a secret forever." He took the gold coin out of his pocket and looked at it lovingly, then held it in front of Cliff's face. "See this? Abraham Lincoln had these minted. He was going to send millions of dollars' worth of these coins into the South after the war to help rebuild. Believe it or not, he was planning on trying to restart the southern economy as quickly as possible." Sherman swiftly pulled the coin away and clutched it tight. "But some people didn't agree with that," he smiled.

"Like William Tecumseh Sherman," Cliff accused.

Sherman smiled and nodded, "Yes. You hit the nail on the head." Sherman grabbed Cliff's chin and yanked his head back and forth. "You're just a regular old Hardy Boy. Do you know who shot Abraham Lincoln?"

Cliff fumed and struggled against his bindings, wanting to jump up and rip Sherman to pieces with his bare hands.

"Oooo," Sherman held his palms up. "You're so tense. Calm down, it's unbecoming. You didn't learn about the Abraham Lincoln assassination in grade school?" Sherman flipped the gold coin into the air happily and caught it again. "Who shot Abraham Lincoln?"

"John Wilkes Booth," said Cliff through gritted teeth.

"Correct! But did you know that Ulysses S. Grant was supposed to be at the theatre with Lincoln that night?" Sherman turned the coin over in his hand. "Instead, he took a last minute trip to Philadelphia. Now let's think. What else is in Philadelphia?" Sherman held the coin up and beamed. "The United States Mint! Within hours of Lincoln's assassination, he had confiscated all of the southern reparations money being held there for what they called 'safe-keeping during such tumultuous times'," Sherman snorted.

"And they were transporting it on the *Sultana* when it sank?" Cliff speculated.

Sherman laughed, "Oh no, the gold was perfectly safe. They put it on a train." He held the coin by his side and fingered it gently. "They blew the *Sultana* up on purpose. Grant and my great-great grandfather, General Willy

T., they were really the ones behind the assassination of Abraham Lincoln. They weren't going to pull the trigger themselves, they needed a willing scapegoat, and John Wilkes Booth fit the bill perfectly. He was an egotistical crazy bastard. They set up the time and place for Booth to kill Lincoln and let him believe that he was on some crusade for justice, but it was all about the money. It's always about the money," Sherman smiled. "Of course, Grant wanted to be president, and he was eventually. Ole Willy T. just wanted the money. He and Grant were real close, serving with each other through most of the war. There were a few others in the top brass who got a cut, but those two took the biggest by far."

Cliff sat in the chair with his head cocked to the side. Was this real? Was he making this shit up? For a few seconds he was even oblivious to the fact that he was still tied to a chair. "Then why try to be so secretive about digging up the wreck?"

Sherman laughed hard. "You thought I wanted to dig it up? No no no no no," Sherman shook his head. "That's funny. I want to keep it from being found. Somehow Booth sensed something wasn't right and made a run for it instead of meeting back up with his contacts like he was supposed to. While he was on the lamb he was keeping a diary. In that diary he wrote down his realizations about the assassination and implicated General Grant and General Sherman. So that the accusations in the diary wouldn't be destroyed if they found him, Booth tore out those pages and mailed them to J.C. Mason, the captain of the SS *Sultana* and a known Confederate operative. The U.S. Intelligence Service carried out a secret mission to sabotage the *Sultana* so that the pages would never be found." Sherman smiled, and flipped the coin into the air and caught it.

"When she refueled in Memphis they planted several coal bombs in the pile that they loaded onto the ship. The wreck took over sixteen hundred lives, but to this day people still think that John Wilkes Booth planned Lincoln's assassination himself. If those pages were discovered, it would be the end of Union Cotton and the ruin of my family. We would become the most hated people in the United States."

Cliff was astonished by what he was hearing. Did all that add up? If it was true, it was the biggest cover-up in U.S. history. That couldn't be the case, could it? Sherman had killed people to protect this secret, surely there was some truth to it. "Wouldn't the pages have disintegrated by now?" Cliff asked.

"The U.S. Intelligence Service had a mole trailing J.C. Mason who eventually worked his way into being Mason's first mate. They knew through him that Mason had a safe, state-of-the-art at the time, that he used to smuggle messages up and down the river. It was proven to be completely waterproof, and the mole documented this. The pages are almost certainly still inside to this day, buried somewhere out in that field across the road. That's why this land is mine, and in a way it always has been. It holds my family's secrets."

"That's why you killed Ronny Millwood and his son?" said Cliff in an appalled tone.

"I had to kill him and that snot-nose boy. He was starting to dig around out there and ask questions. I don't know if you've noticed, but I'm not the kind of guy who likes answering questions." Sherman's lips formed a sick, twisted smile and he had wide dilated pupils. There was a lack of restraint showing in his eyes that was frightening. A chill ran up Cliff's spine but he tried to hide it.

"What did you do with them?" Cliff asked evenly.

"They never left the farm. They're both buried underneath the old pit blind in the timber hole." Sherman maintained his sickly grin as though he thought himself clever. "Nobody will ever find them." He reached behind him and picked up a clipboard from atop the fireplace mantel. "You're going to sign this land over to me now, aren't you Cliff? Or maybe you'd like to join Ronny and his boy, because I can make that happen."

"Like hell I am," jeered Cliff.

"I hate it that you feel that way. You want one more chance to say yes?"

"I'll never sign that."

Sherman breathed in and then exhaled slowly through rounded lips. "Alright. Suit yourself." He took a piece of rope that was lying on the mantel and snapped it in his hands. Cliff's breathing became faster. He watched as Sherman knotted the ends around the middle of a fireplace poker and then twisted the rope into a loop. Cliff's muscles tensed and air coursed forcefully through his nostrils in anticipation of the struggle to come. "You sure?" asked Sherman, looking at him sideways. Cliff stared straight ahead. "Okay," Sherman said, like he was a game show host. Sherman dropped the looped rope around Cliff's neck.

"What's the Gayoso Fund?!" Cliff yelped as the rope touched his collarbone.

Sherman began to spin the fireplace poker, tightening the loop. "Funny you ask, that's actually how I was going to pay you, but you wouldn't take it. You're a little arrogant, Cliff. You shouldn't have been that way, it turns people off." The noose grew tighter.

"Where's the money coming from!?" gasped Cliff before the noose tightened any more.

"I've got many, many coins just like the one I carry around with me stashed in a safe place. They've been passed down secretly through the years, what's left of my great-great grandfather's original share of the horde they stole from the Philadelphia Mint. Millions upon millions of dollars' worth."

Cliff tensed his neck and tried to make it as firm as he could as the rope squeezed down on his trachea. It was getting hard to breath. He took one big, desperate gulp of air.

"Whenever I want to buy some more land and I need a little money, I take a handful of the coins and sell them," Sherman said calmly as he slowly rotated the fireplace poker behind Cliff's head. "They bring a high price, but land is really the world's most valuable and versatile asset. There is nothing else that is truly the basis of power. Gold is just something shiny for people who don't know any better."

Cliff's face was a deep crimson. "Stop," he croaked frightfully.

"You want to sign some papers?" Sherman asked, madly joyful.

Cliff fought for air, his eyes beginning to bug and the blood flow to his brain drying up.

WHAM! At that moment, the front door crashed down and in stormed a team of FBI agents, Zoey Nguyen leading the way. "HANDS UP!" she demanded as she aimed her pistol at Sherman. "Game over."

Sherman grinned and kept his hands on the fireplace poker, the rope taut around Cliff's neck. "I could just leave my hands right here."

"Do that and you're a dead man! It's over Sherman. Give it up."

Sherman just continued to grin perversely and held his hands in place.

"We've already arrested the politicians you bribed, including your buddy Thomas Collins. The gig's up," she said, moving closer.

"It's never up," said Sherman calmly. Cliff gagged and gasped like a fish out of water, about to lose consciousness.

"Put your hands up now and step towards me!" yelled Zoey.

Sherman glared at her and twisted the rope a little tighter.

"Take him down!" yelled Zoey. Two of the agents rushed towards Sherman who rapidly retrieved a stainless steel pistol from under his jacket and pointed it at Cliff's head. The pressure was off the rope and Cliff gulped air, his vision coming and going and his face regaining color.

"Stop or he dies!" Sherman yelled. The agents halted warily.

"It's not worth it, Sherman," said Zoey. "Put the weapon down. There's no way out."

Sherman kept the gun trained on Cliff's head, almost touching his skull with its barrel. With his free hand he pulled the gold coin out of his pocket and clenched it, closing his eyes sensually. He opened them back up and gazed at the coin in his hand with a strange mix of intense pleasure, sadness, and ill-conceived remorse. "Something shiny for people who don't know better," he muttered. He swiftly brought the gleaming pistol to his head and blew his brains all over the living room.

Cliff screamed and shook violently in the chair, splattered with blood. "Get me out of here!" he yelled. "Get me out of here!" The agents stood dumbfounded with their guns down. Zoey closed her eyes and looked away. "Get me out of here!" Cliff continued to convulse, the noose now loosened around his neck. An agent went over to Cliff calmly and solemnly and took the rope off of him, then cut the cords that bound his hands and feet. Cliff rocketed up out of the chair, bolted through the front door, ran across the dirt road in the night, and stood panting under a bright, starry sky in the recently harvested soybean field.

Zoey slowly walked out of the house and approached him. Cliff didn't turn around when he heard her footsteps. "Hey," she said carefully, "you alright?" She stopped and stood next to him, looking out across the huge field.

"Shit, Zoey," Cliff panted fearfully. "I don't know, I really don't know."

Zoey jammed her hands into her pockets, breathed out, and kicked the dirt. "I tried to call you and you didn't answer so we tracked your phone. That's how we found you. We lost the signal after a few minutes. Sherman probably stomped it after it rang."

Cliff continued to stare out into the night, trying to catch his breath.

Zoey looked over at him. "You did good, Cliff," she said quietly.

"Leigh betrayed me," he said.

Zoey didn't know how to respond. She just looked down at her feet. Cliff felt empty, thinking that maybe he should've taken Leigh's offer at Chez Philippe and then never seen her again. How could she have done that to him after everything, after what he had felt? Was it all a lie? Zoey's radio hissed to life. "We found somebody in a storage building behind the house. It's a woman, she's not conscious." Cliff jerked his head to the side and looked at Zoey in bewilderment, and then took off sprinting.

He ran around the house and in the back, outside the open garage door on the front of a white concrete block building, one agent kneeled next to Leigh's body and examined her while another stood beside them and shined a flashlight on her. Cliff skidded to a halt, dropping to his knees beside her body. "Leigh," he supplicated. "Leigh." He touched her face. Her eyes were closed and her hair was tangled but she didn't look any more beat up than she had before. "Is she OK?" Cliff implored to the agent knelt across her body from him.

"She'll be fine when she comes to. She's pretty doped up, though." The agent pointed out the red mark on the side of her neck, "Looks like somebody shot her with a tranquilizer."

"Shot me, too," said Cliff. He picked up her limp hand and held it gently, gazing down at her. In his heart he wildly hoped that Sherman had been lying about her to tear him down. He did everything he could to fight the gnawing mistrust within him.

"This is a classic hostage situation," said the agent. Cliff looked at him. "Had we not arrived when we did, he would've probably killed you and then taken her hostage while he was running from the law. He knew that if the road got short he would need a bargaining chip."

•••

As the dawn was breaking outside, Cliff was sitting beside Leigh's bed in the hospital room, half asleep in the chair. Leigh slowly opened her eyes and glanced around. "Where am I?" she asked, half coherent.

When he heard her voice Cliff perked up, immediately wide awake, and jumped out of the chair and stood beside her. "Leigh!" She lifted her hand up and he held it. "You're in the hospital. Everything's OK. You're going to be OK."

She blinked a few times and grimaced. "How did I get here?"

"You got shot with a tranquillizer dart that knocked you out. Do you remember? They got me too."

"Who? I... why? " she stammered and sat up in the bed.

"Sherman did." Cliff studied her face, trying to detect some sort of giveaway, something to let him know if she really had given him up. Instead, at the mention of his name her mouth gaped, her eyes widened, and she gasped frightfully, "Where is he! How did he find us?"

"He's dead. I don't know how he found us, do you?" he quizzed searchingly.

A look of relief and averted disaster spread over her face. "No," she sighed. "Thank God. I've been terrified. Afraid for the Popes and for you, and I haven't been able to leave their house. I felt like a princess trapped in a castle. I want to go home."

Cliff believed her. Her facial expressions and her voice were genuine. Maybe he was a sucker, but his heart told him that she was telling the truth. "Then let's go," Cliff smiled, and kissed her on the cheek. "Can you get dressed? Do you need some help getting up?"

She shook her head, "No I got it."

"Alright." Cliff picked up the receiver on the room's phone and dialed Zoey's number. "Hey Zoey, It's Cliff. Leigh's up."

"Great!" Zoey said. "She feeling alright?"

Cliff smiled to himself, "Yeah, she's OK."

"Good. Listen, we got the Expedition in the shop. Somebody clipped a homing device underneath the back bumper. It had to be while you were at the prison."

The one-eyed man's face flashed through Cliff's mind. That means Leigh didn't do it! He spun around and looked at Leigh with complete relieved assurance, trust, and affection. She was slipping into her clothes and smiled back at him, like she enjoyed the fact that he wanted to look. "Then take it off," Cliff said offhandedly and smiled at Leigh.

"Well, duh. You sound happy about something," Zoey said.

"Oh yeah. I got a feeling that I'll be spending a lot of time naked in the future. A whole lot of naked."

Zoey laughed. "Bye," she sputtered.

18

The Gayoso House Apartment Building faced the south end of Front Street. It was five stories of red brick and windows. Two wings flanked the front courtyard that Zoey, Cliff, and Leigh walked across to get to the front door. "You're not going to believe this," said Zoey as she opened it.

The trio walked across the bright lobby, down a hall, and Zoey unlocked a heavy door that they went through. Zoey led the way down a flight of stairs, through yet another locked door, and into a large basement room where a dozen federal agents milled about. Some sat at folding tables typing away on laptops and others stood around scribbling on clipboards and collaborating studiously. Zoey waved to them as they walked in, then they turned right and went down another hall. She stood in front of a blank door and looked back at Leigh and Cliff as she gripped the handle. "Are you ready?" she asked excitedly.

"Yeah! Open it," Leigh said with anticipation.

"Are you sure you can handle it?" Zoey smiled.

"Open the door, Zoey!" Cliff laughed.

Zoey pushed the door open. "Ho-ly shit," Cliff gaped. On the other side of the small room a heavy duty and high-tech vault door was swung open against the back wall. In the middle of the vault was a four-foot-tall pile of identical gold coins that shone brightly. Cliff's mouth fell open and he had a hard time registering what he was looking at.

"All 1865 Double Eagles," informed Zoey with a smart grin. They went across the room and entered the vault. Cliff stared down at the pile, dumbfounded. He reached and grabbed a handful of coins to make sure that they were real and let them fall through his fingers; they landed back on the pile with a shower of clinks. Leigh picked up one and held it in her palm and gazed down at it. The left-facing head of the goddess Liberty was surrounded by a halo of five-pointed stars and it was in perfect, lustrous, unhandled condition. "Now we've got to catalog all these," said Zoey. "We aren't even sure how much all this is worth, but it's a staggering number."

"This is unbelievable," stammered Leigh, and placed the coin back on the pile.

"Believe it," returned Zoey. "Now, because this was stolen from the United States Government, it goes back to the United States Government, but it wouldn't be right to leave you two empty-handed."

Leigh and Cliff looked back at Zoey hopefully.

"Both of you reach down and get one. Put them in your pocket. A little souvenir of a job well done," Zoey smiled.

Cliff picked a shiny coin off the top of the pile, held it between his thumb and forefinger, studied it, and smiled as he remembered something. "Can I have one more for a friend?" he asked.

"I guess one more wouldn't hurt," Zoey replied.

Cliff picked up another coin, turned to Leigh, and said, "You and I are giving this one to Brevard Pope."

•••

A month later, the excavation of the *Sultana* was going along smoothly. Archaeologists from the University of Arkansas and the University of Memphis had taken a joint lead on the project. Anthropologists from several other universities were on-site as well, along with a giddy Brevard Pope, who was the unofficial foreman and press liaison on-site. The duck hunting land that had meant so much to Mr. Kenny was now teeming with people, professionals and graduate students alike. Cliff would drive over from Memphis to check on the progress about every other day.

All of the guilty politicians were waiting to stand trial in a case that had turned into one of the biggest scandals in recent political memory. The bodies were found underneath the duck blind and interred in a cemetery near Marion, Arkansas, where the Millwoods had a large family plot. Ronny Millwood's widow was given the option to have the land back after the excavation was over, but she opted not to take it, saying that it held too many memories for her and it would be too painful to go back to it. The land remained in the possession of McIntyre Trading.

The Lincoln cover-up had been big news ever since the story broke. Talk shows covered the new developments nightly, and Cliff had even been approached to write a book about it, which he agreed to with Brevard Pope's help.

The day the safe was located in the captain's cabin, Cliff was working in Memphis. When Pope called him, Cliff quickly drove to the site from his downtown office. When he got there, the rusty, sealed metal pipe sat in a clear plastic box with no lid underneath a big white tent in the middle of the harvested field. Pope and Zoey were both there watching as a middle-aged archaeologist from the University of Arkansas carefully chipped the dirt and rust off of the find. "This safe is incredible; so far ahead of its time," commented the archaeologist. "I cannot wait to get it open."

"This is the last thing I expected," said Pope. "A mutiny of the greatest proportions and the evidence is right here at our fingertips."

"Mr. Pope, I just want to tell you thank you for all your help and support. You're the real reason this got done," said Cliff.

"Just doing what I thought was the right the thing to do—trying to do right by Kenny—but I never thought it would turn into this," said Pope. He turned to the archaeologist. "Are you sure the *Sultana* wasn't carrying any treasure onboard?" Pope smiled.

"We have not found any so far," said the man, "but as the dig continues, you never know. However, I highly doubt that there is anything like that there."

"When will you be ready to open the safe?" asked Pope.

"We will need to take it back to the lab in Memphis before we do that," said the archaeologist. "It will take about two weeks before we reach that point."

"I can't wait to see what's inside that thing," said Pope.

The archaeologist let out a good-natured laugh. "We all feel the same way," said the archaeologist as he looked up from his work. "Just a little bit longer."

•••

Two weeks later the same group, along with the other archaeologists involved with the project and a handful of grad students, were all gathered in a laboratory at the University of Memphis. They had a special guest there as well. Clyde Peterman, now free from prison, was dressed in a nice sport coat and there with his family to witness the opening of the safe. The steel safe had been transported there after it was recovered and had been kept under lock and key. The safe was secured underneath a high pressure CNC machine that cut out metal objects using a high-intensity plasma torch.

"OK is everybody ready? Here we go," said the Arkansas archaeologist, and started the machine. The torch came to life and slowly began to shave off the top of the pipe. It was extremely precise and the cutting went on for about four minutes as everybody in the room watched through their protective eyewear. When the machine cut the cap down so that only a few millimeters or so were left shielding the contents of the pipe from the air outside, the archaeologist turned the machine off.

He put on rubber gloves, went over to the CNC machine, opened it, and with upmost caution, unlatched the pipe from the cutting table. Two assistants were standing by, also wearing rubber gloves, holding a plastic storage bin. Carefully, the archaeologist placed the rusty pipe into the bin. He set it down gently and said, "OK, to the airtight compartment." He held his hands up and said loudly, "Everybody, what we will now do is place the safe into an airtight compartment and open it with a robotic arm. Once the safe is inside the compartment, all of the oxygen will be pumped out of it before we open it. This is so that the one hundred and fifty year old paper will not immediately disintegrate when it comes in contact with the air. We are about to unlock perhaps the biggest secret in American history."

A clear, Plexiglas box was set up only a few feet away from the CNC machine. The box was five feet square and a robotic arm came down into it from the ceiling. The arm had a tiny, diamond-tipped drill bit attached to the end of it, and just below that a high-powered suction cup that operated with the help of a vacuum tube. The two assistants carefully set the plastic bin down on a table beside the airtight box. They opened the back of the Plexiglas box upward and held it aloft while the archaeologist delicately picked up the pipe and set it down inside on two concave supports that had been made especially for this job. The archaeologist then strapped the pipe down gently with metal bands and latched them to hold the pipe in place. The two assistants closed the back of the box, which had a rubber, airtight ring that ran all the way around it, and latched it shut.

All eyes were on the archaeologist, eagerly awaiting what was next. "Now we will pump all of the air out of the box," said the archaeologist so everybody could hear him. He went over to the control panel in front of the airtight compartment and flipped a switch. There was a whirring sound when the pump came on, and it kept going for a few minutes as the archaeologist watched a meter that told him when all the air had been sucked out. When the meter read zero he turned it off.

He turned around to face the people watching. "Now for what we have all been waiting to see. I will use the robotic arm to cut around the circumference of the cap with surgical precision, and then remove it, unveiling evidence of the greatest cover-up in the history of the United States." He turned back around to the control panel and switched on the drill at the end of the robotic arm and it began to spin at an extremely high velocity. Then he pushed a button on the control panel, and the preprogrammed arm moved down and began to cut around the remaining part of the cap on the pipe.

Everyone in the room held their breath for a suspenseful minute as the drill did its work. The bit stopped spinning then the arm retracted the drill bit and attached the high-powered suction cup to the face of the metal cap. The room was tense with palpable expectation as the robotic arm slowly pulled the cap away.

The room was silent and the onlookers breathed shallowly as they witnessed watery, brown sludge sluggishly drip onto the Plexiglas. It fell with the consistency of soured chocolate milk. Their eyes were glued to it and no one dared to speak first. The silence was finally broken when Brevard Pope drawled, "There you have it folks, the evidence for the greatest scandal in American history."

•••

Later that night, Cliff and Pope sat around the oval table in Pope's library. "I just can't believe it," Cliff said. "We were all so sure the pages were there."

"Water will find its way into anything, especially after it has had a century and a half to do it. I guess we shouldn't have been so surprised," said Pope.

Cliff shook his head, "What a find that would have been for the country."

Pope corrected him, "What a find it is, Cliff. Even though the diary pages weren't pages anymore, we still have evidence to support the story. When that brown goop was analyzed it showed remnants of wood particles, which means that there really was paper in there a long time ago."

"You know what I don't understand?" said Cliff. "Why didn't Sherman just give up the secret a long time ago? He died for a story that never would have been proven anyway if he would have just gone ahead and dug up the boat. People wouldn't have guessed that the sludge in that safe was really John Wilkes Booth's missing diary pages. He could have headed the excavation himself, still covered it up, and come off as some big time philanthropist."

"Fear," said Pope. "Simple as that. Fear of the past, of the ghosts that haunt this dark and unforgiving land. In the South, memories tend to linger longer than they do in other parts of the country. Fear influences our decisions more than it should sometimes. He had been brought up to protect the secret at all cost. It had been ingrained into his personality. Sometimes our own family secrets seem as fresh to us as a new wound and as tangible as a smoking gun. I imagine that Walton Sherman tried to deny the truth as much as anyone, I bet he hated it as much a man ever hated anything. He just couldn't come to terms with it, and in the end, for him, the truth was too hard to live with."

•••

Cliff bought an old brick building facing the river on Front Street that he was going to renovate and live in. He was very excited about the project and it stayed on his mind constantly. It was a Saturday morning as he showed Leigh around the empty upstairs, explaining his vision for the renovation. "I'm putting in a bar over here, and keeping all this open," he said with a wave of his hand. "There's a skylight in the ceiling." He pointed up towards the dingy panes. "I'm going to have to redo it. This is where they used to grade the cotton, so they needed a lot of light to see it. Most of these buildings down here have a skylight."

Leigh looked up and nodded. "That will look good," she said like her mind was on something else.

"This floor is going to be mostly for entertaining," said Cliff looking towards the windows, absorbed in his plans.

Leigh looked around at the exposed brick walls. "I like it this way, being here, with you, right now." She grabbed Cliff and kissed him aggressively on the mouth. Her stitches were gone. She pulled her lips away sensually, gave him an inviting glance, and turned her back to him. She pulled her new phone out of the pocket of her jeans.

"What are you doing?" Cliff asked playfully, and tried to peek around her.

She hunched over the phone. "Uh-uh. No peeking. Be patient." She found what she was looking for and smiled and set the phone on the bare hardwood. Leigh spun back around, flipped her hair, grabbed Cliff by the waist, and danced him backwards. They swayed close, their bodies touching, and kissed passionately as Elvis belted *Burning Love*.

Kyle Cornelius is a graduate of the University of Mississippi.
He lives in his hometown of Florence, Alabama.

33254691R10124

Made in the USA
Charleston, SC
10 September 2014